DRAGON RACER

Margaret Bateson-Hill

Catnip

563863

CATNIP BOOKS
Published by Catnip Publishing Ltd.
14 Greville Street
London EC1N 8SB

First published 2008
3 5 7 9 10 8 6 4 2

A CIP catalogue record for this book is available from the
British Library

ISBN 978-1-84647-046-2

Printed in Poland

www.catnippublishing.co.uk

To my children,
Charlotte – Lotty Lupin
Michael – Spiky Mike
Joanna – JoJo
With all my love
Mum xxx

Contents

Part One

DAYS

25 February - afternoon,
Brixton, South London

Chapter 1

Joanna Meets a Dragon

'Come on, Aaron!' Joanna Morris complained impatiently to herself as she looked up the busy high street for her older brother. 'Five o'clock on the steps of the town hall, you said, so where are you?' She threw her school bag on to the bottom step and leaned against the wall. Aaron was *always* later than they had agreed. It was all right for *him*; he enjoyed his after school football club, AND he was always chosen to play in the team. Joanna wished she could find something she really liked too. She'd recently started going to basketball but the only times she ever got chosen for the team were when they were short of players. 'And I know I'm as good as half the girls there!' she'd told her mum.

'Don't worry, next September, when you start secondary school, there'll be loads of new clubs for you to try,' had been her mother's rather unhelpful reply.

Joanna looked up at the clock on the town hall to check the time. Ten past five. If Aaron hadn't come in five minutes she'd go home without him. She stood staring up at the clock as if by watching she could make the giant hands move. Suddenly a movement caught her eye; something on one of the statues near the clock.

'That's a large pigeon,' thought Joanna. She looked again, more carefully this time. It was far too big for a pigeon – *what* was it? And then all she could do was stare up at the clock-tower in utter amazement. Crawling quickly down the wall straight towards her was a small silver dragon!

The dragon stopped and looked at her intently with its bright eyes shining like two small bonfires. Joanna stared back. She could see herself reflected in the dark pupils; only instead of her school uniform she seemed to be wearing a fitted leather jacket, the sort motorbike riders wear. The dragon's face was now so close she could feel its hot breath on her cheeks. She reached up to touch it. Suddenly thoughts like small silver sparks were flickering across her mind, '*Dragon Flyer*' they cried and were gone, only to return brighter and faster. Now her head was spinning and she had to lean against the wall of the town hall to stop herself from falling. She looked up just in time to see a woman scoop the dragon up into the thick folds of a blanket. It all happened so quickly that it took Joanna a couple of seconds to realise that the woman with the blanket was already disappearing through a side door. Joanna ran after her but at the same moment she heard her brother calling her. 'Jo! Wait,' and Aaron came running up. 'Mr Wentworth wanted to sort out all the details for the match tomorrow... guess who's captain! And then Matt and I needed to discuss tactics. ... hey Joanna, you're not listening. Are you all right, you look a bit funny?'

'I don't know, I feel a bit strange,' replied Joanna, adding silently, 'you might too if you'd just discovered a dragon waiting for you!' Because she was sure it *had* been waiting for her ...

As they walked home all Joanna could think about was the dragon's face and its round fiery eyes. But however amazing, there was no way she was going to tell Aaron what she had seen. If she said she'd seen a dragon crawling down the wall of the town hall he would either laugh at her or worse, want to hang around and see it for himself! And she certainly didn't want *that*. This was her secret and one she needed to think about before she told *anyone*. Luckily Aaron was still so wrapped up in all the details of his football match that he wasn't paying her much attention. They walked slowly up the road together until Aaron shouted, 'Race you! Last one home does the washing up.' Joanna found herself shoved into a garden wall as her brother raced passed her.

'Cheat ... I'm not doing your washing up, do your own.' She pushed past him into the house, trying unsuccessfully to slam the front door behind her.

'Oi! What's up with you?' he shouted, but Joanna had already disappeared up the stairs into her room.

'Why are you arguing with your brother?' Joanna's mother called up the stairs. 'What's the matter *this* time?'

'Nothing's the matter,' thought Joanna to herself. 'Except ... I've seen a dragon!' She lay down on her bed and closed her eyes. It was such a wonderful secret! Just *knowing* made her feel so different. Would anyone be able to tell just by looking at her that something amazing had happened? She went and stood in front of the mirror. She *looked* exactly the same as before – long brown straight hair (still in school plaits which she instantly pulled out) and brown eyes. A small girl – well, smaller than everyone else in her class and pretty, even Joanna knew she was pretty. She took a step closer to the mirror and whispered to her image, 'I've seen a dragon!' She stared deep into the reflection of her own eyes as she tried to remember the dragon's.

'Dragon Flyer.' The same silver sparkly thought came flitting through her mind – only louder this time. She looked around startled and a bit frightened, almost expecting to see somebody standing just behind her.

'Dragon Flyer' – what did that mean? Certainly the silver dragon she had seen at the town hall had wings, not that it had used them. Joanna realised she knew very little about dragons. Even when dragon racing was headline news on the telly she'd never paid much attention. Some boys in her class were really keen on them and were always going on about some sports programme they watched every week– but it was on a premium pay per view channel. Still she was bound to find out lots if she looked up dragons on the internet. She went down stairs only to find her dad already sitting in front of the computer tapping away at the keys.

Joanna frowned. 'Are you going to be long Dad, because I need to use the internet?'

Without looking up, her father said, 'I must finish this piece of work tonight; I've got an important deadline you know.'

Joanna knew all about her dad's important deadlines. Sometimes she thought that her dad didn't actually do anything at work all day, but just brought everything home. He was always tapping away on the computer, or talking business on the phone.

'What is it you want to know about?' asked her dad.

'I'm doing a project on dragons ... for school,' Joanna lied. If she didn't say that her father wouldn't take her seriously at all. He would certainly never believe that his own daughter had been eyeball to eyeball with a dragon that very afternoon.

'Dragons!' said her dad. 'Interesting! But instead of doing facts and figures like everyone else – why not do dragons in fiction? Go and look on the bookshelf.'

'What! So I won't disturb you on the computer – that's what you mean, isn't it?'

Anthony Morris stopped typing and turned to look at his daughter. She could tell he was cross. 'Joanna, just get on with your work and then I can be left in peace to get on with mine.'

'I need the computer too,' said Aaron coming

into the room. 'Dad, I've got to download this file from school; otherwise I can't do my science assignment.'

'Well, hurry up then,' said Anthony Morris, making way for his son. Joanna looked at the pair of them in astonishment. 'You always do that – let Aaron do *his* stuff. You never let me do mine.' 'But I've already helped you – told you to go and look in those books,' her father replied. 'And anyway Aaron gets more homework than you.'

'Oh yes, and he's so perfect!' Joanna slammed the door behind her as her mum come running out of the kitchen. 'How dare you speak like that to your father?'

'Dad should say sorry to me,' retorted Joanna. 'He let Aaron go on the computer, when I asked first. And of course, darling, perfect Aaron's homework MUST come first.'

'I'm sure your father was trying to help you *both* – and Aaron has got more homework; but it seems to me that if you have enough time to go winding your father up, then you'd be better employed doing something useful – like setting the table. You've done nothing but argue with everyone since you came in.'

In the end Joanna's evening was completely spoiled. Everyone blamed her when her father stormed into the room claiming that all the interruptions had so upset his concentration that he had turned off the computer without remembering to save his work. 'But I didn't touch the computer,' argued Joanna.

'Joanna, I have had just about enough of your behaviour. Up to your room now! And I do not want to hear the word "dragon" again this evening,' said her father crossly.

Joanna stormed up the stairs into her bedroom. 'It's not fair; why do they ALWAYS blame me!' she shouted to the girl staring angrily back at her from the mirror. 'Nobody ever thinks ANYTHING I say is important. Well, now a dragon has noticed me and I'm going to make sure I find it again.'

Joanna threw herself on to her bed and began to think what to do next. Beyond the hum of traffic, she could hear the clock of the town hall strike nine. 'The town hall – that's the place to start! And what about that woman who caught the dragon in the blanket? If I can't find the dragon I might be able to find her. It's Saturday tomorrow, so I'll be able to go first thing. And then I'll go to the library and find some books on dragons.'

All she could do now was wait for the morning.

Chapter 2

A Day at the Races

One week earlier – a small island off the coast of Cornwall

Vincent Marlowe, owner of the Brixton Dragon Caves, climbed out of the helicopter, stretched his long legs, carefully folded his coat over his arm and walked away from the landing pad.

The island, normally uninhabited, was crowded with racegoers. Vincent breathed deeply, almost tasting the excitement in the air. Conditions were perfect and the clear light of the winter sun meant everyone would get an excellent view of the races – especially from the new stand with its panoramic view over the small bay.

As he looked around, Vincent felt old and out of

place. The hospitality tents that had sprouted like strange colourful flowers on the green hillside were teeming with crowds of smart young professionals more interested in being photographed for the pages of some glossy celebrity magazine than watching the racing! He noticed with surprise that most of the tents were marked 'for members only'. 'Members of what?' he wondered.

He looked around again; nothing seemed to be in its usual place. He wasted a good ten minutes trying to understand the colour-coded signs for the different amenities before a steward came and explained them to him. It was all a far cry from the days when Vincent had first visited the island with his flask of coffee and tin of sandwiches.

There was still a little time before lunch so he joined the crowd admiring a new spectator stand. A representative from the World Dragon Racing Federation (WDRF) was proudly informing everyone about the design and cost of the stand, with its new plasma screens for watching the races. Along the top of the stand he could see an impressive display of the flags of the participating caves. In the centre, flew the flag of the current champions, the Brighton Pavilion Caves. In fact the silver and red flag with its golden crown seemed to be everywhere. Vincent frowned. The gold and black flag of his own Brixton Caves wasn't there! It had to be a mistake! It was traditional to represent ALL the dragon caves racing on the day.

Vincent marched back to the welcome desk. The receptionist smiled politely as he voiced his complaint.

'Well, Mr Marlowe, I am sorry you feel *your own* cave has been under represented. So far we have received only favourable comments about the new facilities and decorations. If you want to make a complaint you'll need to fill in a form.'

She pushed a slip of pink paper and a pen at Vincent and turned away.

Realising he would get no further help Vincent took the form. 'I don't suppose I will even get a reply.'

He was determined not to let the incident spoil his day, and decided that a spot of lunch would lighten his mood. He chose a quiet table in one of the smaller refreshment tents and sat down to read the programme, which gave full details of the breeding history and the current form of the dragons racing that afternoon. Vincent scanned quickly down the list until third from the bottom he found the name of the dragon representing the Brixton Caves: a Welsh Red dragon called Cadwallader. This would be the dragon's last race, as his flyer, Harry Campbell, was leaving to join a new dragon cave that had recently opened in Cornwall as part of a European Community's Enterprise Initiative. Cadwallader was too set in his ways to tolerate another flyer and, like all dragons his age he was beginning to put on weight. Still, the dragon was already guaranteed a new home with a fabulously wealthy rock star who was suffering similar problems of weight gain and aging.

The dragon's retirement left Vincent with something of a problem. Although he was hatching a new dragon egg, for the rest of the current season there would be no dragon representing the Brixton Caves. It would be the first time he hadn't finished a season. 'Not that many people will notice,' Vincent thought, with just a hint of bitterness. 'Perhaps I should retire too – draw a line under this part of my life.'

Vincent stared despondently down at the plate of food and pushed it away. He wasn't feeling hungry anymore. Was this where all his hopes for the day were leading him – to give up dragon racing? Well then he'd better go and take his seat for the races – it might be the last time …

By the time Vincent had managed to find the entrance that led to the seating for dragon cave owners there were only a few minutes left before the start of the races.

'You can't go up there until I've checked your pass.' A large uniformed man stood in the entrance to the stand, blocking the way.

'I'm sorry,' said Vincent, somewhat taken aback. 'I've been coming to the races for over forty years and I've never needed to show my pass before.'

'New security regulations, sir,' replied the doorman importantly.

'Of course,' said Vincent, courteously. He took a leather wallet from his pocket and pulled out a small card, showing his photograph embossed with a serial number.

'I'm sorry sir, but this is not the appropriate pass for *this* stand.' The doorman handed back the pass.

This second refusal made Vincent angry and bewildered. 'But this is an owner's pass. Look here's the official WDRF stamp and serial number.' He pushed it back at the doorman. 'Hurry up and let me through, the races are about to start.' Vincent stepped forward to go through the entrance, but the doorman stepped in front of him. 'I shall have to call security if you continue to be a problem.'

Vincent was shaking with anger. This day was turning into one long nightmare. 'Call security then. 'They'll soon tell you that I am Vincent Marlowe, owner of the Brixton Caves. In all my long years of racing I have never been treated like this.'

'Is something the matter, doorman?' said a voice from behind Vincent. He turned to see Marius King, owner of the Brighton Pavilion Dragon Caves, surrounded by an entourage of business associates and personally-invited guests. The doorman immediately stood to attention. 'Nothing to bother you with, sir. Why don't you go straight through, the race is about to start? I'm just about to call security.'

Marius King walked slowly up to Vincent Marlowe, shaking his head. 'Dear, dear! Didn't you know that the categories for the passes have been changed? Surely you received notification from the WDRF?' He pulled out his own pass and waved it in Vincent's face.

Vincent stiffened. 'No,' he replied firmly, 'I did not.'

A cruel smile flickered over Marius King's face. 'Perhaps they thought you weren't coming – *do* you have a dragon racing today?'

Vincent did not reply. Marius King stepped closer. He was a tall well-built man, but Vincent noticed with some satisfaction that he still had to look up to meet Vincent's eye. Marius King laughed aloud, revealing perfect white teeth. 'Let me explain, *this* stand is for owners who have actually *won* a race this season – and you haven't had a winner for some time! Although what is it you're quoted saying in this month's *Dragon Fire* – Oh yes! "*The sheer beauty of a dragon in flight is its own reward!*"' He continued – 'Don't let me keep you; I'm sure you'll find the view from the new *visitors'* stand will still allow you to appreciate the finer points of dragon flying. Doorman, perhaps you'd care to show Mr Marlowe the way.' But Vincent had already gone.

Vincent could still hear Marius King's mocking laughter as he walked away. He was so angry that he hardly noticed where he was going. He was vaguely aware of the cheering shouts of the crowd. The first race must have started then, but everyone already knew who the *winner* would be. The dragons from the Brighton Caves had won all the major races this season. Vincent wasn't sure why he'd even bothered to come. Obviously the WDRF already regarded him as a *'has-been'*!

'Hey, Mr Marlowe, not going are you? The races have only just started. Why not have a drink with me, give me the chance to talk a few things over with you.' Vincent was surprised to see that the young man calling over to him was Mike Hill – known in the trade as Spiky Mike. Vincent knew only two things about him: his infamous quick temper and the fact that he was the most talented of the new generation of dragon trainers.

'Not much point in staying really. I have to face facts. I am an old man who is finding it difficult to come to terms with the way that the world of dragon racing is changing.'

'Just a bit of show Mr Marlowe, to make people feel important – don't let it get you down.' Spiky Mike pulled out a chair and gestured to Vincent to take a seat, 'I expect you've seen a lot of changes?'

Vincent nodded 'Too many to count … but it's only today that I realise … well, you may as well be the first to know I'm thinking of retiring.'

Spiky Mike looked so shocked that Vincent couldn't help feeling pleased. He stood up to leave but to his astonishment Spiky Mike grabbed his arm. 'Mr Marlowe – you can't retire! Not now!'

Vincent gave a sigh. 'Kind of you to say so, but really nobody would have noticed if I hadn't come today.'

'That's where you're wrong, Mr Marlowe. *You* were the very reason I came today and before you go, you must hear what I've got to say.'

'How can I refuse?' said Vincent astonished by

the young man's outburst. 'But I can't imagine how I can be of any assistance to you.'

Spiky Mike pulled his chair closer. When he finally spoke, his voice was so quiet that Vincent had to lean forward to hear him. 'What I am going to tell you, Mr Marlowe, has already made me a number of powerful enemies. But sometimes you have to speak out whatever the personal cost.' Startled, Vincent looked across at the young man. Until recently Spiky Mike had been head trainer for the Brighton Pavilion Caves. It had been widely reported that he'd left in a hurry. Vincent knew he was about to find out why.

Spiky Mike looked around to check nobody else was listening before he said, 'For sometime now, Marius King has been carrying out a series of top secret experiments in the hope of creating the perfect racing dragon. But the experiments went horribly wrong and two dragons were abandoned in a disused cave, which is where I found them. One was past help and the other – well let's just say the other one is now in safe hands. I reported it to the WDRF, but Marius King made up some story about some mystery ailment afflicting a couple of his dragons and the necessity of quarantining them. Of course the WDRF fell for it hook line and sinker, especially when his colleague,

Dr Alexander, came forward with paperwork confirming everything.'

Vincent listened in astonishment.

'What did you do next?' he asked.

'I was so angry I asked for the case to be reopened, but the WDRF said that if I made any further complaints I would face disciplinary action, perhaps even lose my trainer's license. After that I didn't feel like taking a new job immediately – wasn't sure if anyone would employ me. Instead I decided to do some research into the old histories of dragon racing to see if they could help me find a way to challenge Marius King.' Vincent sat up with a start. 'What did they tell you?'

'I soon discovered that in the earliest records the times were even faster than now – but I couldn't discover the reason why – until just recently I came across an article that said the earliest dragon racers were all … alchemists.'

Spiky Mike looked cautiously across at Vincent before he continued.

'Tell me, Mr Marlowe – do you think that some of the secrets of dragon racing are hidden in their writings?'

Vincent looked back across the table at Spiky Mike. 'Now why would you think I might know the answer?'

Spiky Mike returned Vincent's steady gaze with his own. 'If I remember rightly, you are a scholar – a scientist in your own right. In fact you are known in dragon racing circles as "The Alchemist". But that's not just a nickname for you, is it?' Spiky Mike's voice fell to a whisper. 'Am I right in believing that is exactly what you are?'

Outside the tent the crowds started cheering wildly, signalling the finish of the first race.

The two men didn't move until the noise had died down. Finally Vincent Marlowe, returning Spiky Mike's questioning gaze with a small smile, spoke, 'And if I am an alchemist?'

The fact that he had not denied it gave Spiky Mike confidence to continue. 'Help me find a way to challenge Marius King. Find out what those early dragon racers did, Mr Marlowe; search through all your books and stuff or whatever it is you do.'

Before Vincent had a chance to reply Spiky Mike suddenly stood up and said in a normal voice, 'Nice to chat with you, Mr Marlowe, and I'm sorry you missed the race.' Vincent looked up to see Marius King's dragon trainer, Afra Power, watching them. She turned quickly away and disappeared into the crowd.

Immediately, Spiky Mike turned to Vincent.

'Look I've got to go, but if you discover *anything* let me know. You can contact me on this number.' He gave him a card and disappeared out of the tent.

Vincent sat there for sometime thinking over the events of the afternoon. 'I wonder!' he said to himself. Feeling refreshed at last, he stood up and left.

Chapter 3

The Egg Turner

24 February - evening, Brixton

With the departure of his flyer, Vincent Marlowe was left with only one employee – his faithful friend Agnes Thomas. Despite her seventy-two years, Agnes was still as keen and as eager to work as she had ever been. She was an Egg Turner and her job was to turn the hatching dragon's egg twice a day – once in the morning and once in the evening – during its fourteen months of incubation.* It

---

*   The turning of the dragon's egg is an essential part of rearing a dragon suitable for racing. Years of breeding and research have proved that to produce the fastest, sleekest racing dragons, a dragon's egg needs turning twice a day.

was a highly-skilled job that needed a steady hand and a careful eye; a good Egg Turner was a valuable asset in the world of dragon racing.

When it was time for the second turning of the day, Agnes took the keys from their hook and walked slowly along the main passageway until she came to the small door that marked the entrance to the nursery caves. Its ancient timbers were embellished with a curious pattern set in iron and gold. She unlocked it and went inside. The caves themselves were lit by the soft glow of oil lamps set into the walls. Agnes walked briskly past cave after cave until she came to the smallest of all – nothing more than a small hollow carved out of the rock. Inside the hollow lay a box. Putting on a pair of thick blue fireproof gloves Agnes carefully lifted up the lid. A large silver egg was suspended in the middle of a ring of fire. Taking a pair of tongs from a hook on the cave wall she turned the egg over. Then she closed the lid and adjusted the dial that monitored the temperature of the box by turning it up one extra degree. 'Won't be long till you're hatched, just one more turn,' she whispered. Back in her office she took out the large register where she recorded the details of each egg turning and added – 'Estimated time of dragon hatching 1.30 pm, 25 February.'

The entries were written in the black ink of a fountain-pen, old fashioned these days when so many of her counterparts in other caves were turning to the computer.

This would be the eighty-ninth dragon born in the caves since she had first become an egg turner nearly forty years ago when she had arrived in Britain from Jamaica. Then the Brixton Caves had been known as the very best in the country.

As she turned over the pages looking at the entries she smiled to herself each time she recognised a familiar name. As an egg turner she had the privilege of naming the dragon whose egg she'd turned. Agnes knew the names of all *her* dragons – but she was especially proud of those that had won one of the major races: Tennyson, Aristotle, Scholastica and her own personal favourite, Zephaniah!

Agnes sighed. She had enjoyed the hustle and bustle of the busy caves. Now she was the only one left! She couldn't really blame Harry for leaving, he was still young and he honestly believed the promise of a job in a modern computerised dragon cave was too good an opportunity to pass by – not that she would ever have wanted to work in such a soulless place. Vincent, generous as ever, had released Harry from his contract although it had left him without a flyer. Despite appearances, Agnes knew Vincent had taken Harry's departure very badly. Then last week he'd returned from the races like a new man. He'd disappeared into his study saying, 'I need to do some research and I do not wish to be disturbed!' She'd hardly seen him since but she knew he was happier than he had been in years. Why, she'd even heard him singing to himself!

Agnes put the register away. She got her coat and bag and locked the door behind her. She was just about to call out, 'Goodnight, Alchemist,' when there he was standing before her. His eyes were fiery and bright with excitement.

'Agnes, would you mind terribly staying a little later this evening. I have made a remarkable discovery! Please come into my study.'

Agnes followed him down the long corridor, her curiosity growing at every step.

The study was tidy, just as it always was. To her right was the desk. On it was a collection of parchments in a neat pile. Beside them lay an inkstand and a pen. Behind the desk, filling the wall was a collection of old leather bound books. Every shelf was labelled and numbered. On the wall to the left was a large glass cabinet that held scientific apparatus. Agnes sat down on the chair opposite Vincent's desk and looked across at him. He was such a tall thin man that when he sat down his knees seemed to reach up to his chest. With his small round, bearded face and dark bright eyes that twinkled though his gold spectacles he always reminded Agnes of an owl perched up in a tree – a well dressed owl to be sure, in a dark suit, white shirt and highly polished black leather shoes.

'My dear Egg Turner, it was here all the time just waiting to be rediscovered and now I've found it!' He held up a roll of parchment for her to see.

'What is it?' Agnes asked mystified. The parchment was covered in writing, but the lettering was so ornate that she couldn't make out a single word.

'I believe,' Vincent's voice dropped to a whisper, 'that this is the original manuscript of *Ova Draconum* written by the greatest of the 15th Century Dragon Lords, Magnus Crascus. Here he recorded for the first time all the important processes of egg turning. Even our most recent reference books still follow the process described here.'

'An original manuscript? How fascinating!' said Agnes, hoping she was showing enough enthusiasm. 'I expect it must be very valuable. Thank you for showing it to me.' Agnes stood up to go. 'Vincent, could I look at it tomorrow? It's just that I need to go now before the shops close.'

'Go? Now? But I haven't told you yet!' said Vincent, jumping up from his seat.

'Told me what?' said Agnes, feeling very bewildered; she had never seen him so agitated.

'Vincent, are you all right?'

Vincent came round the desk and took hold of her arm. Agnes could feel him trembling. 'My dear Egg Turner, I have never felt better in my life!' He returned to his side of the desk and carefully spreading out the parchment in front of them began to explain, 'Over the years this manuscript has been translated many times over for use by Egg Turners everywhere. But what if those translations were, through ignorance, open to misinterpretation?'

His voice rising, Vincent pointed down at the parchment, 'You can see quite clearly that throughout the document Magnus Crascus uses the usual word *ignis* for fire, until that is, this final part of the document – here – where he refers to fire as *spiritus draconis,* that is 'dragon's breath'. Now, in modern translations that has been interpreted as …'

'Steam – or rather the temperature at which water becomes steam, 100° C,' said Agnes.

'Correct … but Agnes, that is not what Magnus Crascus meant at all!' said Vincent excitedly.

'Are you sure ,Vincent?' asked Agnes, 'All these years I have followed the procedure as described in my reference books and the dragons have always hatched properly ...'

'I thought I must be mistaken too – until I compared the flight times of dragons in the earliest records. Agnes, we've never seen speeds like them!'

'But surely someone else would have discovered it before now. Why only last year the WDRF brought out a new revised edition. I have a copy and it's really excellent.'

'Oh, I'm sure they are right *as far as* their knowledge goes. But ...'

'What? Vincent, you are talking in riddles!'

'Agnes, everyone knows that Magnus Crascus was the most famous dragon lord of the Renaissance, but what is not commonly known is the fact that he was an alchemist ... and *only* another alchemist would recognise the *true* meaning of his words – that *spiritus draconis* is the purifying fire of alchemy ...'

Vincent held out the manuscript and slowly began to read, ' "*An egg placed in the dragon's breath for its final turning will be purified of all excess. The dragon born from such a flame will be sleek and fast, the perfect manifestation of physical flight.*" '

They both sat perfectly still. Suddenly in her

mind's eye Agnes could see a dragon in flight – and such a dragon! Vincent was smiling as if he could see it too. 'Wouldn't you like to try such an experiment with that egg you've been turning? What if I were to make such a fire?'

Agnes sat there open-mouthed. 'Wouldn't you have to be an alchem ...' She stopped, and gazed at Vincent as though she was seeing him for the first time. 'You are one, aren't you, and there was I thinking it was just a nickname when all the time it was true!'

'I should say *was*; I haven't practised for years. – I don't need gold and I haven't made the elixir of life since my dearest Maud died ... I couldn't save Maud, so what was the use.'

Agnes sighed. She remembered Vincent's pretty young wife, killed in a car crash so tragically all those years ago. Why, it had happened only a few months after Agnes had started work at the caves. Vincent had been out of town at the time and when he arrived at the hospital it was already too late.

'Vincent, are you sure you want to make this fire?' Agnes asked as gently as she could.

'Yes I do!' said Vincent, 'I really do! But you have turned that egg for over a year, so it must be your decision too. Of course, if the experiment fails, there will be no dragon. Perhaps you need time to think about it before you make your decision. Tell me, how much longer until the dragon egg is ready for its final turning?'

The question brought Agnes back to the present. 'Oh my goodness! Why, Alchemist, the next turning will be the last!'

'What! So soon? Then we must decide now, my dear Egg Turner.'

Agnes sat for a moment looking down at her hands in her lap. 'It seems to me, Vincent, that some decisions are made for you. In the Bible we are told, 'To everything there is a season.' I think you were meant to find that manuscript just at this time; so I say, make your fire, it's about time we had a winner in the caves again.'

Vincent laughed excitedly. 'And I'll buy you a new hat especially for the occasion.' But he added seriously, 'Thank you Agnes! Thank you for being there and not losing faith.'

'So will the egg turning be at its usual time of 7.30 tomorrow morning?' asked Agnes getting up from her chair.

'Indeed it will,' replied Vincent. 'So go home and get a good night's sleep. We're both going to need a clear mind and a steady hand tomorrow.'

Chapter 4

The Dragon is Born

25 February – morning, Brixton

When Agnes arrived for work she found a hand-written list of instructions from the Alchemist waiting on her desk. Agnes carefully read through the instructions twice; this was a crucial moment for the dragon's egg and nothing could be left to chance. The instructions informed her that Vincent was busy preparing the fire. She was curious to know if it would look any different from ordinary fire. She glanced down at her watch. It was still only 7.15. She busied herself tidying her already tidy desk, and then with another glance at her watch she took the keys to the caves from the hook, and stood patiently waiting by the door as the final minutes ticked by. At 7.25 she opened the door and made her way to the smallest dragon cave where she put on the blue fireproof gloves. It was 7.30. She took the box out of the hollow, wrapped it in a blanket and walked out of the caves.

The study door was already open. For a moment Agnes stood still in the doorway, hardly daring to move. Straight in front of her, in the great fireplace, there now blazed a fire – but such a fire as she had never seen before! The flames shone with an intense silver brilliance that cast strange shadows around the room and Agnes watched the light softly reflecting off Vincent's glasses, making them shine like silver coins. He turned to her and smiled.

'The fire is really quite something, isn't it Agnes? Do you know, when I woke up this morning I was suddenly quite nervous about whether I could still make it.'

Agnes found it difficult not to keep staring at the flames as she walked over to where Vincent was waiting by the fire.

'Take out the egg, Agnes,' were his simple instructions. Knowing she needed to concentrate on the task in hand, Agnes turned away from the fire to place the box on a small table. Only then did she lift up the lid and carefully pick up the egg with a large pair of tongs.

'Put it in the fire.'

'Wouldn't you like to, Alchemist?'

'As Egg Turner that task belongs to you.'

Agnes carefully placed the egg into the fire. It looked almost invisible, as it lay cradled in the silver whiteness of the flame. For a moment she stood completely mesmerised by its extraordinary intensity. As the flames licked the curves of the egg she found herself dreaming of the white sandy beaches and the long hot hazy sun-filled afternoons of her childhood …

Vincent gently took Agnes by the hand and led her away from the fire to sit in his own great chair. 'I had forgotten how powerful the flames can be for those who have never seen them before. Why don't you go to your office and fill in the egg turning register? I'll call you for the hatching.'

Still feeling dazed Agnes made her way carefully over to the door, where she turned to look one last time at the egg hanging suspended in the fire. Having felt the power of the flame she couldn't help but wonder what sort of dragon would emerge from the egg.

Experience told Agnes that the dragon would start hatching exactly six hours after the last turning. Sure enough at 1.30 p.m. she heard the small tinkling bell that meant she was needed. She hurried down the passageway and found Vincent peering in to the fire. She could sense his excitement. 'Look – a large crack has just appeared across the centre of the egg.' Agnes stared into the flames and saw the egg start to shake violently from side to side. Small cracks were spreading over the surface until suddenly it burst open, sending splinters of shell in every direction. A small creature lay motionless in the flames as if in breaking open the shell it had exhausted itself. The dragon was born.

Just a few moments lying in the heat was enough to restore it to full vigour and it started to stretch open its perfectly formed wings. Immediately, Vincent, who had been watching intently, took the pair of tongs next to the fire, picked up the dragon by its long thin tail and dropped it into a glass cabinet on his table. Then he promptly shut the lid. The dragon immediately started to beat its wings against the glass sides. 'We've done it,' cried Agnes. 'Yes!' said Vincent, hugging Agnes, 'I really think we have!'

'Frisky little one, isn't it,' laughed the Egg

Turner. 'I'll take its details – if it stays still long enough!'

She picked up her notebook, took out her black fountain pen and started to write.

'Date: 25 February. Time: 1.36 p.m. Weight?'

Agnes waited whilst the Alchemist lifted the glass cabinet on to a set of scales. The needle swung round violently and then came to a standstill. For a moment they both stared at the numbers on the dial hardly daring to believe they could possibly be true. 'But if you minus the weight of the cabinet then the dragon only weighs 4.12 kg!' stammered Agnes incredulously.

'It's truly remarkable!' nodded Vincent, smiling down at his old friend. 'The dragon is carrying no excess weight!'

Agnes's hand trembled with excitement as she noted down all the details for the dragon register. 'Vincent, my writing is not what it should be. It's just that I can hardly believe … why the dragon … he's quite wonderful.'

Somehow Agnes managed to complete the necessary paperwork that would inform the WDRF that this particular dragon was a male, Silver Spiked-Back. She noted that along the side of the dragon was a faint thin black line ending in a point like a spear and copied the markings on to a small outline of a dragon printed in her notebook.

'And now', said Vincent, 'last but not least, what name have you chosen for the dragon?'

'I spent all last evening thinking of a suitable name; after all, this is a very unusual dragon. His name will be ... Excelsior – used by the poet Longfellow as "an expression of incessant aspiration after higher attainment."'

'Excelsior! A fine name – we must never stop trying to get better at what we do. Excelsior! I like it very much. Now Agnes, if you wouldn't mind filling out his birth certificate and registration documents for the WDRF, I'll take him down to his cave for his first meal.'

Picking up her notes, Agnes returned to her office to fill in the official documents. Once these were sealed and addressed she hurried off to the post office. Only on her return did she notice the note propped up against a small vase of flowers. It read:

Dear Agnes,
I telephoned Spiky Mike to tell him about the birth of Excelsior. As you can imagine he is very excited. At present he is out of

London visiting an old colleague
in Wales but he says he'll drive
back tonight so that he can see
Excelsior first thing tomorrow
morning. As a result I have
rescheduled another appointment
to early this evening. I should
be back by eight but I would
be grateful if you could check
Excelsior before you go. He is in
cave number 1. See you tomorrow.

Vincent

Agnes looked around the office with a sense of satisfaction. The caves were alive again with a new dragon and a new trainer! How things had changed! 'And then there will be the arrival of a new flyer! I wonder who it will be,' mused Agnes. With Spiky Mike as trainer they would probably be able to take their pick from a whole host of flyers. 'Well, luckily that's not my decision,' thought Agnes as she washed up her tea cup. 'Goodness, it's ten past five already. I must check Excelsior.' She took down the silver keys to the nursery caves and went down the passageway. When she reached the cave she stopped and stared. The door to the caves was open. She quickly made her way to cave number 1. It was empty. Where was the dragon?

*　*　*　*

Later that evening Vincent came back to find a very worried Agnes. 'All I could think was that he'd escaped. I grabbed the blanket I keep in the office for egg turning emergencies and hurried off to find him. Luckily, he had not gone far. He was crawling down the wall of the clock-tower, and I was able to catch him in the blanket.'

'I suppose we must be thankful he hadn't flown further,' Vincent sighed. 'But Agnes, did anyone see Excelsior? If word gets out that a newly-hatched dragon escaped from the caves we could be hauled up before the WDRF for disregarding health and safety regulations. Section 4 still stresses the need for discretion as far as the general public is concerned.'

Agnes looked at Vincent. 'What, even though every race is shown on television.'

'My dear Egg Turner, watching dragon racing from the safety of your home is one thing – coming face to face with one, however small, in the high street is altogether different. So Agnes, please put my mind at rest – did anyone see Excelsior?'

'Oh dear, Alchemist, I'm afraid someone did.

It was a young girl – she was about ten or eleven,' said Agnes.

'Not the sort of person to report us then,' smiled Vincent in relief. 'Now you have had a long and tiring day, why don't you go home … and Agnes – thank you!'

Chapter 5

Trouble

26 February - Brixton

As soon as Agnes arrived at the caves the following morning she knew there was trouble. Vincent's study door was wide open and Vincent was nowhere to be seen. She found him standing guard at the entrance to the nursery caves. He had dragged some heavy boxes across in an effort to keep the doors closed. Even now something was banging against them. 'Agnes, thank goodness you're here; Excelsior is trying to get out again and I don't think I can hold him back much longer. Go to my office and find the bottle of dragon-freeze. It should be in the third drawer of my desk ... and please HURRY!'

Agnes was back in an instant with a small spray bottle. She handed it to Vincent who allowed the door to open just enough for him to squeeze his arm through the opening. He gave a couple of squirts of the bottle and waited for the thump as the dragon fell to the ground, stunned by the spray. Together they pushed the boxes to one side, and then, opening the door, they saw the silver body of the dragon lying helpless on the floor.

'Quick, Agnes, open the door to cave 12, the lock on that door is much stronger.'

Even with Excelsior securely locked up, it was a very worried Vincent who told Agnes how Excelsior had been in the middle of eating his breakfast when the dragon had suddenly kicked over the bucket of chicken livers and had tried to fly up to the top of the cave. 'I was most alarmed by this extraordinary behaviour so I hurried out of the cave and shut the door behind me; but Excelsior attempted to follow me and I had to barricade him in. Luckily you came just in time to help me.'

Agnes listened in silence but finally she said, 'I've never known a dragon react quite like this. What if he escapes again? We're not as young as we were; perhaps we're not quite up to handling Excelsior?'

Vincent sighed. 'I've never experienced anything like it before either and I can't say that I am *not* worried. We'll just have to keep a close eye on our young friend until Spiky Mike arrives. Let's hope he can shed some light on his behaviour.'

*   *   *   *

Joanna stood underneath the clock-tower and looked up. She tried to remember where she had first seen the dragon and the way it had crept down the wall towards her. Could it be lying hidden on a ledge? Above her, giant stone-women returned her gaze, but kept the secrets of what they saw hidden behind their silent lips. Where should she look next? The side door where she had seen the woman with the blanket take the dragon was locked. Joanna sat down on the town hall steps. She hadn't found any clues to help her solve the mystery of the dragon, but she was not going to give up. The dragon had found her yesterday, and sooner or later she knew he would come and find her again. In the meantime she would just have to find out as much as she could about dragons! Looking across the road she saw that Brixton Library had just opened.

*   *   *   *

By the time Spiky Mike arrived Excelsior had returned to normal, but the trainer knew exactly what the problem was.

'Well, that's that then!' he announced dramatically, as he tore up the piece of paper in his hand. The small white pieces fell to the ground like snowflakes.

'What do you mean?' asked Vincent anxiously.

'That was a list of people I thought we should consider as flyers for Excelsior. I don't need it any more,' said Spiky Mike.

'Is the dragon ... untrainable? If word gets out that we have a maverick dragon on our hands it would be the end!' Vincent had to sit down as the sickening feeling in his stomach almost overwhelmed him.

'Untrainable! Whatever gave you that idea? No, the dragon is fine, in fact he's wonderful!' Spiky Mike went over to the cave wall where the dragon was lying curled up as though it were asleep – except that Spiky Mike could see a glint of an eye watching him from under the silver slip of eyelid.

'So my friend, already you're full of surprises – and I guess this will just be the first of many. I don't know if I should be pleased or not ...' Spiky Mike turned back to Vincent and Agnes.

'Who's the dragon met? Who visited the caves last night?'

'Nobody did,' said Vincent, 'why do you ask?'

'Because Excelsior has already chosen his flyer and is trying to reach them.'

'What! How do you know?' questioned Vincent.

'Very early on – I must have been about 16 – my Dad got me some work experience with the dragon trainer – you probably remember her – Elizabeth Anne Kelly? She'd been retired for years, but she always took an interest in new trainers trying to get a foot on the ladder.'

'Elizabeth Anne Kelly! I remember her,' replied Agnes. 'Wasn't she known as Loopy Lizzy?'

'I know what people called her!' said Spiky Mike, 'but if you ask me that woman was a genius. OK, so some of her ideas were strange, but she had an instinct with dragons – especially for finding the right flyer. But, and this is really the point I want to make, I remember distinctly her telling me, that very occasionally a dragon would – on some whim known only to itself – choose its own flyer. *"And whatever you do, do not interfere. You must allow the dragon to make immediate contact with its flyer. Failure to do so puts everyone in the cave at risk".*'

'I thought at first she was winding me up until she told me she had witnessed a dragon bring down the roof of the caves in its attempt to be reunited with its flyer. The question is, who can it possibly be? Who can Excelsior have chosen?'

Vincent stood shaking his head in disbelief.

'Are you really sure this is the case? I mean, Excelsior has only met you, Agnes, myself … and … oh surely not …'

'What do you mean *surely not*? Who?' Now it was Spiky Mike's turn to sound worried.

'A girl saw Excelsior crawling down the town hall!' replied Agnes. Spiky Mike turned to Vincent with a look of horror on his face.

'Tell me you're joking! How? When?'

'It happened yesterday afternoon, just after I'd gone out,' Vincent admitted reluctantly. 'Agnes caught him very quickly, but not before a girl had seen him. Do you think *she* is the chosen flyer then?'

'Who else could it be?' groaned Spiky Mike. 'And we have no choice but to try and find her – and quickly.'

Vincent sat down and tried to think what to do next. If this young girl was really Excelsior's flyer, he would need to approach not only her, but her family. And if they didn't find this girl soon it would only be a matter of time before Excelsior escaped again.

'But how to find her! I'm presuming she's a local girl, but she might not be.'

'Excelsior will be able to find her wherever she is,' said Spiky Mike.

'But we can't just open the door and let Excelsior fly off,' interrupted Agnes.

'I didn't mean that!' snapped back Spiky Mike. 'What kind of idiot do you take me for?'

'Please, my dear friends,' said Vincent. 'Let's keep calm about things. We have to find some way of getting Excelsior to show us the way without anyone else seeing him. Now let's all of us just sit quietly and think.'

After a few minutes Agnes suggested, 'My granddaughter has an old baby buggy.'

'A baby buggy?' scoffed Spiky Mike. Vincent decided to ignore him.

'What do you mean, Agnes?' he asked.

'We could hide the dragon in the buggy, wrapped up in a blanket and see which way he wants us to take.'

'Do you think it would hold Excelsior?'

'I think it would. He's about the same size as a toddler; and with the rain-hood down no one would see very much.'

Vincent turned to Spiky Mike, who was looking dubious.

'I think we should give it a try – though perhaps we should wait until after dark. Very well Agnes, could you go and get it immediately? While you are gone, Spiky Mike and I will try and make some sort of plan and think over what we are going to say to this young lady and, more importantly, her parents!'

*　*　*　*

Although the buggy was a good, large, solid one, they decided that they would keep Excelsior knocked out with dragon-freeze until they were out on the street. They strapped him in as best they could, tucked blankets around, and pulled down the hood.

But Spiky Mike shook his head. 'This is going to go terribly wrong, I just know it. Those straps won't hold him if he wants to get out. I'd feel better if he were on a chain as well.'

Finally, just before seven, chained and wrapped in blankets, the dragon was as hidden and secure as they could make him.

'I suppose we'll find out soon enough if our little plan is going to work!' said Spiky Mike giving Excelsior one last spray of dragon-freeze as they made their way up from the caves.

'Which way first, Vincent?' asked Agnes. 'Up the High Street or Brixton Hill?'

'Hurry up and choose quickly,' said Spiky Mike, who was pushing the buggy, 'that dragon-freeze is already wearing off, I can feel him pulling at the straps.

'Up Brixton Hill then,' said Vincent. But immediately the buggy started to shake so violently that passers-by began to stare.

'Quick! Try the other way!' directed the Alchemist. Spiky Mike spun the buggy round. Immediately the dragon inside stopped moving and Spiky Mike gave a sigh of relief. 'It looks like it's this way. Come on.' They made their way along the still-crowded high street and were just about to cross a side-street when the buggy began to shake again. Spiky Mike turned into the side-street and again Excelsior became quiet. Their journey continued in the same way with Excelsior shaking the buggy violently at every wrong turn, until a few minutes later they found themselves standing outside a mid-terraced Victorian house. Vincent turned to his two colleagues.

'Well, here we are. This must be the home of the young lady in question. Let's hope the second part of our plan is as straightforward as the first.

Agnes, if you could knock at the door – and make sure they can see your official WDRF badge.'

The door was opened by a pleasant-looking woman. She smiled questioningly at Agnes. Agnes smiled back. 'Good evening, madam I am sorry to disturb you. My name is Agnes Thomas and my colleagues and I here are members of the World …'

'Oh, I'm sorry,' interrupted the woman, the smile fading fast, 'but we aren't interested in hearing about your church. Thank you very much. Goodnight.' And she closed the door in Agnes's face.

Agnes turned round in amazement to Vincent and Spiky Mike, who were still waiting by the gate. 'Oh dear, she thinks I'm trying to convert her. Perhaps you should have a go, Vincent?'

The Alchemist walked up to the door and knocked loudly. This time they heard a chain being slid into place, before the door opened. 'Sorry, we really aren't interested,' came the woman's voice.

'We're not from a church and we're not selling anything,' called the Alchemist, 'my name is Vincent Marlowe and I am the owner of the Brixton Dragon Caves. We would like to speak to you about your daughter and the possibility …'

The woman interrupted, 'Look I'm not

interested and if you knock again I'm going to call the police.' She closed the door firmly in Vincent's face. Spiky Mike kicked the wall in anger. 'Now what do we do? That stupid woman won't listen at all. Look, she's watching us through the curtains. We'll have to think of something else.' Spiky Mike turned the buggy around and started to walk back down the road, but as he did the buggy started to rock violently from side to side. From inside came the sound of ripping fabric and before any of them could do anything to stop him, Excelsior burst out from under the hood, wrenching the chain from Spiky Mike's hands. The dragon flew straight up to an open upstairs window and disappeared inside the house, leaving three stunned and horror-struck people below.

Chapter 6

That's a ... Dragon!

26 February - evening, Brixton

Joanna was lying on her bed reading *Dragons in Norse Mythology* when she'd heard the first knock at the door. She was feeling very comfortable and didn't want to move. It was probably just her dad and brother coming back from football. Then she heard a second knock, her mother's raised voice and the front door being slammed shut. She'd just put down her book to go and find out what all the fuss was about when suddenly she heard her mother screaming in terror. At exactly the same moment a flash of silver came flying through her open window stopping her in her tracks.

Could it possibly be …? Turning slowly round she let out a cry of delight. Yes it was! It was the dragon … somehow it had found … HER. To be precise it had landed right on top of her making her fall over with a crash. For a moment she lay there unable to move. The dragon lay still on her chest, its wings folded back against its silver body. Even through her thick sweater she could feel heat from its belly. Shaking with excitement, Joanna lifted up her head so that she was looking directly into the dragon's face, its bright fiery eyes almost dazzling her and then she nearly jumped out of her skin for she distinctly heard the words, 'Hi-ya flyer! Making contact with you has been trickier than I'd thought. I could feel you calling me, but your instructions were unclear! However, contact has now been established and all will be well.' Joanna could only lie there with her mouth opened wide in astonishment. The dragon was talking to her, not out loud but rather inside her head. It continued, 'You don't need to speak, if you just think your thoughts I'll understand you and you can understand me. Like if it's not comfortable for you with me sitting on your chest, I'll move!' At that the dragon launched itself up into the air and Joanna was able to stand up. At the same moment her bedroom door opened and there was her mother screaming hysterically 'Joanna, Joanna, get away! That's a … that's a … dragon!' The word 'dragon' seemed to affect Hilary Morris terribly. She let out a little whimper and fell in a dead faint in the doorway.

'Hey! Is she frightened of me?' The dragon's words came tumbling in to Joanna's head in a flurry of excitement. 'How thrilling! I quite like the thought of people fainting in terror at just one glimpse of me.'

'Actually you're really quite sweet,' said Joanna. 'I think she fainted because finding a dragon in your house is quite a scary thing for most people. In fact, I've just been reading about some really fierce greedy ones who like to eat princesses for dinner.'

'Oh, do we really get to eat princesses!' responded the dragon excitedly, 'I've only had buckets of chicken livers so far. Joys to come!'

Joanna and the dragon went over to where Hilary Morris lay limp and insensible on the floor. Joanna patted her mother on the cheek trying to get her to wake up. 'I think I'm supposed to stick her head between her knees or something so that the blood rushes the oxygen to her brain.' As Joanna pushed her mother into position she heard her give a low groan and her eyes fluttered. 'Ooh, I think she's coming round!' cried the dragon. 'Let's see!' and before Joanna could stop him he'd flown down to Hilary Morris. She chose that moment to open her eyes; gave another scream and promptly decided the unconscious state was the one she preferred. 'Whoops no, not yet! She's gone again,' said the dragon.

'Excelsior, leave her alone! It's you she's scared of!' shouted Joanna. 'Oh! Your name, it's Excelsior. How did I know that?'

'Well, I thought it was about time we got on to first name terms. So I *thought* it to you. Your name is Joanna, better known as Jo to close friends. But if it's all right by you I'll call you JoJo. You can call me XL if you like! And if you're worried about your mother, well we can go and ask the Alchemist what to do about that. I must say she's looking positively green, isn't she? I expect Agnes will have something in her bag to make her better and then you can all have a nice cup of tea. I never touch the stuff myself.'

'The Alchemist? Agnes? Who are they?' asked Joanna.

'They hatched me, so I suppose they're the closest thing I have to parents, and they are standing outside your house at this very moment, along with Spiky Mike, wondering what to do.

Let's open the door and let them in.' Relieved to escape Excelsior's chatter, which left her feeling quite dazed, Joanna stepped carefully over her mother and went down the stairs to the front door. Standing by the gate were three people, so engrossed in discussion that at first they didn't notice her. 'Excuse me,' called Joanna, 'I think you'd better come in. My mum's just fainted. She's a bit shocked about Excelsior and I'm not quite sure what to do next.' With a look of utter relief on all of their faces that events inside the house were not as bad as they had been imagining, Vincent, Agnes and Spiky Mike followed Joanna into the house.

'Where is your mother, my dear?' asked Vincent.

'She's lying on the floor of my bedroom. It's at the top of the stairs at the front. She will be all right, won't she?'

'Oh yes, Agnes here knows exactly how to deal with cases of shock such as these.' Vincent turned to Spiky Mike. 'Will you go and help Agnes revive this young lady's mother and I will explain who we are and why we are here.'

'Just one thing,' replied Spiky Mike as he followed Agnes up the stairs, 'where's that dragon gone?'

Automatically Joanna replied, 'He's up in my

room lying on my bed – oh how did I know that?'

'Told you so,' Spiky Mike called back triumphantly to Vincent. 'She's a natural!'

'A natural what? Joanna, who are all these people? And where's your mother?' said Anthony Morris marching through the open front door at exactly the wrong moment. Joanna's heart sank. 'Oh no' she groaned to herself, 'Dad and Aaron!' She looked from her father to the tall suited-man and back again. Never in all her daydreams about finding the dragon again had she EVER imagined it would be like this!

'Oh, hi Dad, you're back early, um … this is Mr … um … Mum's fainted and they are helping me.'

'What! Where is she?' cried her father, aghast.

'Upstairs!' Her voice came out in a tiny squeak.

Anthony Morris ran up the stairs past Spiky Mike. Joanna was about to follow as well when she felt a hand on her shoulder. 'Probably best if you and your brother stay down here. Let's go and sit down.' Vincent followed the children into the sitting room. Almost immediately Spiky Mike came back down the stairs leading Anthony Morris. He was opening and closing his mouth very slowly and uttering funny noises that had no meaning.

'Ah,' said Vincent 'It appears he has met Excelsior. How is the mother?'

'Agnes is bringing her round now,' replied Spiky Mike.

Up till that moment Aaron had been standing dumbfounded, watching the extraordinary events unfold. But at the sight of his own father reduced to a quivering wreck he turned angrily to Joanna. 'Who are these people? What's the matter with Mum and Dad?'

Fortunately for Joanna, her father announced in a loud voice,

'Joanna, there is a dragon asleep on your bed. Aaron, there is a dragon asleep on your sister's bed.'

Aaron turned with a stunned look to his sister, 'Jo, what's Dad talking about?'

'It's true Aaron, there's a dragon on my bed, and it belongs to these people. It flew in through my window this evening.'

'If I find out you're winding me up, you're dead!' shouted Aaron as he walked up the stairs. Joanna started getting the tea things ready, and waited for her brother to return. In two minutes he was back. 'OK, I'm sorry I didn't believe you – the dragon's brilliant, brilliant ...' To Joanna's surprise she saw that her brother's eyes had gone all misty. He turned away, adding quickly, 'By the way, Mum's come round now; so you can bring over the tea.' Joanna carried in the tea things to find everyone gathered in the sitting room. Her mum and dad were sitting side-by-side on the sofa. They were both very pale. Beside them sat Agnes. Aaron went to sit in the best armchair while the young man, Spiky Mike, was standing by the window. By the fireplace, with all eyes fixed upon him was the tall man. What had Excelsior called him? Oh yes, the Alchemist.

On seeing Joanna, Vincent smiled. 'Ah, there you are, my dear! Yes, bring in the tea and then I shall explain what this is all about.'

Joanna handed round the cups and then sat on the floor at her parents' feet, her heart pounding. The dragon had come to find her, and now she would find out why.

Two hours later the world of Dragon Racing lay open to the Morris family! Vincent Marlowe had given a brief history from the origins of Dragon Racing in the 14th Century to the present racing season and the various 'Dragon Caves'. Agnes spoke of her job as an Egg Turner and finally Spiky Mike told them about the necessity of matching a dragon with a particular flyer. 'Which brings us to your daughter, Joanna!' smiled Vincent. 'Normally a dragon flyer is found within the world of dragon racing; as you can see, meeting those outside is fraught with problems. However, the dragon Excelsior has, for reasons of his own, chosen Joanna. So we now come to the case in point. Mr and Mrs Morris, will you give permission for Joanna to train as Excelsior's flyer?'

Joanna's heart skipped a beat – she couldn't believe that she'd heard Vincent correctly – that the dragon had chosen *her*, Joanna, as its flyer? That they would race against other dragons. Could it really be happening? No one *ever* chose her for anything. Ever! She looked up at her parents, hardly daring to breathe. They were looking rather blankly at each other; until her father said, 'But Joanna's just a young girl. Quite ordinary really ... I mean ... surely you need to be the strong tall athletic type?'

'I *am* growing and I can do loads of exercises to get stronger,' interrupted Joanna.

'At the moment all that concerns me is whether or not you will allow Joanna to train as a flyer,' replied Vincent. 'Perhaps you'd like time, as a family, to think about it.' He spoke quietly and patiently, but it occurred to Joanna that underneath it all Vincent was very anxious. Spiky Mike was starting to pace up and down the room, whilst Agnes sat there with her eyes closed. 'They must *really* want me!' thought Joanna. But what if her parents said no? Unable to contain herself a moment longer she cried out, 'Oh please, please say yes. I'll do anything! Mum! Dad! Please!'

'Well, I don't know,' started her father. 'What about the costs? I mean it might all be very expensive!'

Vincent smiled. 'All expenses will be paid for by the Brixton Dragon Caves.'

'What about her school work?' added her mother.

Then suddenly Aaron burst out, 'Oh don't be silly! Of course she's got to do it. You're always going on about Joanna doing something that she really likes and when the very best thing EVER comes along you start talking about school and stupid stuff.' Joanna couldn't believe her ears. Aaron had never spoken up for her like that before! She jumped up and hugged him, 'Oh, thank you! Thank you!'

'The boy's right,' remarked Spiky Mike, 'all you have to do is say yes!'

Anthony Morris turned to his wife, 'I don't think we could stop her even if we wanted to – which I don't, do you?'

'No,' his wife smiled weakly, 'in fact it might even be fun.'

'Well, Joanna, if that's what you really want.' Anthony Morris turned to Vincent. 'OK, the answer's yes!'

Joanna couldn't help it; she leapt up into the air – higher than she'd ever jumped at basketball. 'Oh, Mum! Dad! Can I really? Oh thank you! I just can't believe it! I'm going to race dragons …'

She just had to hug everyone – her mum, her dad, her brother, Vincent, Agnes, even the young man, Spiky Mike! And to top it all her dad let her have a small glass of champagne which he brought out to toast his daughter and her new friends.

As for Excelsior, he was blissfully asleep on Joanna's bed and even though she was downstairs Joanna was quite sure that she could hear him snoring!

Chapter 7

Advancement

26 February - evening, Brighton

That very same evening Marius King leant back into the softness of his black leather chair and let his eyes sweep quickly over the group of people sitting around his boardroom table. All attention was fixed upon him, awaiting his every word. He took time to enjoy the moment; knowing he was the perfect picture of wealth and power. He wore his success like a second skin along with his designer suit and expensive watch. Funny how a few accessories made it so easy to get people to do *exactly* what he wanted. He had a talent for that – getting people to do what he wanted. Early in his career he had discovered that a little flattery and a few vague promises worked wonders (especially if he kept quiet about any unwanted truths that might get in the way). And now here was another wonderful opportunity to put his talent to work. He flashed a broad smile and began.

'Before I tell you why I have asked you here today, I want to offer each one of you my congratulations. Why? Because you *are* the best in your own specialised branch of Dragon Racing. And the project I have devised not only requires but also *deserves* the best. It is my intention to harness your talent and create the ultimate Dragon Racing Team!' He allowed himself a brief pause to savour the ripple of excitement that ran around the room.

'Good! I sense your excitement! Our work, here at the Brighton Pavilion Caves, is already acknowledged to be at the cutting edge of technological advancement. There are *those* of course who aren't ready for such developments; inevitably *their* only response is to accuse me of cruelty to dragons.' He shook his head and smiled a knowing smile at his audience.

'I would rather suggest that there is no progress, no real achievement without risk and this work will certainly not be for the faint hearted so if you're not prepared for 100% total commitment now is the time to go.' Nobody moved.

'Good! So let's get straight on to business. I would particularly like to welcome our two new investors who have underwritten all the financial costs of this project. Let me introduce media mogul, Sir Donald Morton, and, on behalf of the Saracen International Bank, Ms Edelweiss Araz who has flown in from Switzerland especially to be present at this meeting.' He turned to his guests. 'In return I would like to introduce *to you* the team who will be spending your money! First let me present Dr Frederick Alexander, not only the chief Egg Turner, but also an eminent neurologist.' He gestured towards a thin balding man in a white coat who briefly lifted his head to acknowledge the visitors before returning to his notes. 'Dr Alexander will be overseeing the physical development of the dragon. On his right is Afra Power, newly promoted to the position of Head Trainer. She will be working exclusively on this project.' There were nods of approval all round.

'A strong team, but useless without the jewel in our crown – our new Dragon Flyer. His family needs no introduction in the world of dragon racing since his mother was the first African-American woman to become supreme champion. She is, of course Marion Claverdale, whilst his father is the industrialist and tycoon, Conrad Oliver. Afra and I recently visited him in the States to put him through his paces. Let me tell you he is exceptional. My friends, let me introduce via satellite, Hannibal Henry Oliver.' Marius King flicked a switch and an athletic, good-looking young man appeared on a huge screen on the wall.

'Hi everyone, it's Hannibal; Stateside they call me H_2O – cool but essential!'

Marius King smiled back at the screen. 'Hannibal, we are all looking forward to meeting you very soon. I've just been telling everyone here about how impressed we are with you. But I know that, like everyone here, you want to know about your dragon. Let me promise you it will be very special. Stay with us now and come and witness its birth.' Marius King turned to Dr Alexander.

'Frederick, I believe it's time to make our way to the birthing unit!' Dr Alexander took out his palmtop. 'Indeed it is. By the time we get there the first cracks should be starting to appear.'

Everyone followed Marius King along the corridor to the birthing unit, Egg-Turning Laboratory 3. Dr Alexander tapped in a code and the stainless steel door slid open. A furnace containing the dragon's egg lay directly in front of them. They could see it suspended in the flame through a large plate-glass window. Small cracks were beginning to show on the surface of the egg.

Marius King turned to his audience. 'Dr Alexander has already been developing new genetic technologies in the breeding of the egg. As you know, it is essential to regulate the ratio of fat to muscle, to ensure power and speed. In previous experiments he has been able to alter a dragon's genetic code to enhance the development of wing muscle, but as a result the metabolic rate of the dragon had been slower than usual, causing the dragon to put on weight at an alarming rate. To counteract this Dr Alexander has started to experiment on the dragon's brain itself. Frederick, perhaps you would like to continue.'

Dr Alexander pushed his glasses up his nose.

'Using detailed information from a magnetic resonance imaging scanner I have learnt how to rewire a dragon's brain so that I can strengthen certain functions such as perception and communication whilst minimalising such problems as unnecessary weight gain. By using this information alongside new genetic technologies I have been able to change the chemistry of certain molecules whose purpose is to guide the nerve fibres or axons that connect the brain's 100 billion neurons. As a result, I am able to guide the axons to neurons in whatever part of the brain I choose.'

'It all sounds very complex,' commented Ms Araz, 'are there any side effects?'

'All further questions will have to wait Ms Araz,' said Dr Alexander raising his hand. 'Ladies and Gentlemen, please be silent and watch; the dragon is about to hatch.'

The dragon's egg could be seen through the glass window shaking violently. Then all of a sudden the shell exploded showering fragments all over the inside of the furnace. Dr Alexander pressed a series of buttons. Immediately the newly born dragon was lifted out of the furnace and placed in a clean and very large glass cabinet ready to be exhibited to its audience.

Everyone stared through the glass at the motionless emerald green-scaled body. At first the dragon didn't move, then very slowly, the dragon's wings started to unfurl until the full span of wing was completely extended and the tip of each wing was touching the sides of the glass. Spontaneously everyone present started to clap. 'Wow!' came Hannibal's voice from a nearby screen. 'That's a Jewel Dragon. I never knew you could race Jewel

Dragons and look at those wings – spectacular! Boy, it's gonna be some ride. When can I start?'

Afra turned to Marius King looking very alarmed. 'A Jewel Dragon? You didn't tell me it was going to be a Jewel Dragon. You do realise how aggressive they are?'

Marius King shook his head and laughed softly. 'Afra, haven't you been listening to anything Dr Alexander has been saying. He can rewire the nerves in a dragon's brain in any way he now chooses. He can transform all that aggression into speed, just you wait and see.' He turned again to his guests. 'There'll be plenty more surprises for all of us before we've finished. Now let us leave Dr Alexander to finish recording the details of the dragon's birth. 'Hey,' came the voice from the computer screen, 'aren't you forgetting something?'

'And what's that, Hannibal?' Marius King couldn't quite hide a slight impatience in his voice.

'Why, its name of course!'

Marius King allowed a huge smile to spread over his face. 'How could I forget? Dr Alexander, I realise that traditionally it is the job of the Egg Turner to name the dragon, but would you kindly indulge me and allow me the honour of naming our new arrival?' Dr Alexander was already busy with his instruments. 'Of course! Such traditions are meaningless to me.' Marius King walked back to the glass cabinet. 'I have known for a long time what this dragon's name should be. As a child, one story in particular caught my imagination – my hero defied the gods by stealing from them the gift of fire. The dragon will be named after this great hero – Prometheus.' As if in answer the dragon beat his wings against the sides of the glass and from its mouth came a small jet of flame.

Marius King led his guests out of the room leaving Dr Alexander to his calculations.

The last to leave was Afra Power. At the last moment she turned back to the cabinet. Could it really be true that Dr Alexander had found a way of controlling a Jewel Dragon? She couldn't help but wonder what Spiky Mike would think of it all – not that she was on speaking terms with him. Even now she still shuddered every time she thought about that dreadful afternoon when Spiky Mike had walked out of the caves. How he'd asked her to leave with him … and the look on his face when she'd refused. The row that followed had been terrible. 'But you had no right to accuse me of selling out, Mike. I was just doing my job. And as for trust! I thought *our* relationship *was* based on trust. But there you were sneaking around the caves like some vigilante. And where were these dragons so cruelly treated by Marius? I never saw them and nobody else found anything suspicious in the caves. Let's face it Mike, you never saw eye to eye with Marius over anything even when you first took the job.' Afra sighed. It didn't seem to matter how many times she went over the arguments in her head she always came up with the same answer – that the only problem in the cave had been … she hated to say it … *Spiky Mike* himself with his moods and his temper! She missed him though – more than she ever let on to anyone in the caves … 'And why couldn't you understand that I've worked too hard to get where I am just to give it all up because of one unproven accusation?'

She looked through the glass at Prometheus. He was quite the most spectacular dragon she'd ever seen. 'So here's my challenge,' she whispered, 'to prove you wrong, Mike.'

Chapter 8

Mind-Blending

5 March - one week later, Brixton

'Oi! Jo! Wake up! Come on, Mum says you've got to get up NOW!' Joanna suddenly felt Aaron's voice forcing her to wake up. 'Go away!' she muttered 'It's Saturday ...'

Saturday! She felt her stomach give a little leap and she was instantly awake. It was Saturday! At last! After what had seemed like the longest week ever, *today* she was going to start her training. Joanna didn't have the faintest idea what the training would involve; Excelsior was far too small to carry her, but still today was the day.

'I'm surprised you're still in bed,' said her

mother as she came into Joanna's room with a pile of ironing. 'After all the fuss you've been making all week about not being able to wait until Saturday, I thought you'd have been the first up. This is going to be quite a commitment so I think you should say right now if ...'

'Mum, don't be stupid!' Joanna jumped out of bed and started throwing on her clothes. 'I just found it difficult to get to sleep' – she didn't dare add that until three o'clock in the morning she hadn't slept at all – 'see, I'm ready now.' Joanna tried to slip past her mother, who quickly closed the bedroom door. 'Not so fast! You're not going in those old jeans and when you've changed, you need to make sure your bedroom's left tidy *and* that you bring down your school uniform to be washed or you won't be going anywhere.'

'You never make Aaron do all this before football,' muttered Joanna to herself – today was obviously not the day to make such a complaint out loud – the last thing she wanted was her mum to change her mind about the dragon racing.

But despite her threats, Joanna's mother did not change her mind and at ten o'clock, just as arranged, Joanna and her parents arrived at Lambeth Town Hall. Vincent was already waiting for them on the stone steps.

'Good morning Mr and Mrs Morris, good morning Joanna! I thought you'd enjoy coming in through the main entrance, as this is the first time you've visited the Brixton Dragon Caves. Normally we use the side entrance so as not to draw too much attention to ourselves.' They followed Vincent up the steps and through a wooden door labelled 'Private'. They continued along a short passage until they came to the doors of a lift. Both Joanna and her parents gave an 'ooh!' of delight as the lift doors opened. The walls of the lift were covered in panels of finely wrought gold metalwork showing flying dragons. Their descent was swift and smooth and the lift doors slid silently open to reveal a large circular hall, softly lit by a huge crystal chandelier suspended from a flying dragon. Vincent stepped out of the lift and turned to his guests,

'Welcome to the Brixton Dragon Caves!' For a moment they could only stop and stare, for the entrance hall of the Brixton Dragon Caves was decorated to impress. They stepped out into a circular hall, its creamy silk walls covered with huge golden-framed oil paintings of dragons. Vincent led them through a pair of doors into a wide and very long corridor lined with brightly lit glass cabinets, from which shone countless trophies and cups. Interspersed between the cabinets were photographs of dragons with their flyers. Joanna stopped to examine one of a very young-looking Vincent standing next to a very sleek, but powerful-looking dragon. Underneath she read the words 'Scholastica – Winner of the New Year's Day Derby 1957'. Half way down the corridor Vincent turned and opened a door into what looked like a huge library. Each wall was completely lined with books. 'Wow,' said Joanna. 'There are nearly as many books in here as in the library across the road. How many have you read?' 'Most of them, actually' replied Vincent. 'Please feel free to borrow any you wish.' Joanna looked a bit aghast. 'Oh I'm not sure they're my sort of books!' Vincent laughed. 'Probably not until you are a little older, but I didn't bring you in here to choose books, but to meet Spiky Mike.' Spiky Mike was sitting on a chair in the middle of the room looking slightly out of place in his jeans and t-shirt. He grunted a 'Good morning,' followed by, 'Ready for work, Joanna?' Joanna nodded excitedly. 'Of course.'

'Meanwhile Mr and Mrs Morris, let's go to my study to complete the forms to register Joanna as a trainee flyer,' smiled Vincent. 'I'll also take you through the timetable of events we have drawn up and answer any of your questions.' As they disappeared back into the corridor, Joanna turned expectantly towards Spiky Mike.

'Right Joanna, I want to make it quite clear from the start that this is not a game. Flying a racing dragon is hard work. Vincent and your parents are insisting, for the time being at least, that you stay on at school. However that doesn't mean *I* shall expect any less from you. During term time, your training will take place on Saturdays and Sundays. On top of that you must come and practise for at least one hour after school every day. There'll also be longer training courses in the school holidays.'

'He could make it sound a bit of fun,' thought Joanna to herself, adding aloud, 'I do know I've got to work hard.'

'Good, I'm glad I've made myself clear. Let me start by telling you that, luckily for us, as far as the flyer is concerned, dragon flying is not about physical power, but mental power. Dragons are certainly physically powerful, but ultimately they are creatures that control through the cleverness of their minds. You have already seen how Excelsior communicates with you using telepathy.'

'You mean, when I can hear his thoughts in my head and he can hear mine?' Joanna asked.

'Exactly,' said Spiky Mike, 'that's a dragon's normal way of sending and receiving messages.

But if you want to *fly* a dragon to race it, then you have to go one step further – you have to mind-blend with it.'

'Mind-blend? What do you mean?' asked Joanna, curiously.

'It means you have to learn to merge your thoughts with the dragon's, so that you fly as one.'

'Is it dangerous?' asked Joanna, somewhat alarmed at the thought. Mind-blending was not the kind of thing she had imagined at all. She'd had visions of endless keep-fit exercises to build up her muscles, not her brain.

'Not if *you* do as *I* say. Don't forget it is a gradual process. Now when we enter Excelsior's cave, I'm going to ask you to go and sit next to him and to rest your face against his. You'll feel his thoughts immediately, but it's important right from the start for you to show Excelsior that you are his equal and that you won't let him overwhelm you. He will also be testing you to make sure that you aren't going to dominate him either – it's really about trusting each other. That shouldn't be too difficult because Excelsior is a Silver Spiked-Back dragon. Their breed is ideal for racing. They're sleek and fast with a strong desire to win. But they're also good-natured as dragons go – in fact almost friendly.'

'Well, that's OK then,' thought Joanna sarcastically to herself. Did he have any idea how nervous he was making her feel?

Obviously Spiky Mike did not, for he continued. 'Now the mind-blend consists of four simple questions and all you have to do is telepathically communicate them to the dragon. The first three are preparatory and the fourth is the invitation. As soon as Excelsior replies, ask him the next question. If he doesn't reply, you must say, 'Please tell me.' Keep asking the question until he tells you. There'll come a point when he will refuse to answer you. Don't give in. He's probably testing you to see how you will react – you need to be firm. Of course he may also become over-excited and try and overwhelm you with chatter. The same rule applies. Don't boss him and don't apologize. Just repeat the question.'

He took a piece of paper from his pocket and handed it to Joanna.

'Here are the questions. Have a read through and don't look so worried. It's not too hard.'

Joanna read through the four questions on the paper. They seemed simple enough, but … 'Can't you show me how it's done?' asked Joanna.

'Not with a racing dragon,' replied Spiky Mike. 'It's important to get a really good, strong partnership going. I promise you within a few weeks it'll be as natural as breathing.'

'OK!' said Joanna out loud, but thinking 'I haven't a clue what you're talking about.'

There was one question she felt she *must* ask. 'How do I stop mind-blending?'

'To break the mind-blend you just ask the first three questions and then thank the dragon for mind-blending with you. Come on, I'd like to make a start this morning.'

Without giving Joanna a chance to say, 'What! Now?' Spiky Mike jumped up from the sofa, opened the library door and set off at a brisk pace; Joanna had to run to keep up with him as he turned off the main corridor. She found herself in a long high passage that appeared to be carved out of the rock itself. She was suddenly aware that she must be hundreds of feet under the ground. It was a very strange feeling.

Spiky Mike opened the doors to the dragon cave and she followed him in. Although it was dark, Joanna could sense she was in a very old cave that must have been formed thousands of years ago. She felt her heart give a little skip; sitting in the middle of the cave floor, bright and alert, Excelsior was waiting for her. The silver dragon was more beautiful than she'd remembered him and much larger too: in that one week he must have doubled in size. The fiery brightness of Excelsior's eyes was the only light in the cave, but they shone so brightly that around the dragon there was a small pool of brightness.

She heard Spiky Mike's voice from the shadows behind her. He spoke barely above a whisper.

'Walk slowly up to Excelsior.'

She walked slowly forward, unable to take her eyes away from the silver dragon.

'Sit down beside him and lay your head against the side of his face. Take your time.'

Joanna could feel her legs trembling beneath her as slowly she sank down next to Excelsior. His belly was warm, whilst his neck and face were cool. Carefully, she leant her face against his and felt the pattern of his scales surprisingly smooth under her cheek. Beyond the small pool of light there was nothing but darkness. Next to her, Excelsior was still and quiet. She heard Spiky Mike's voice continue, 'Joanna, keeping your cheek against Excelsior, begin to ask the questions.' Joanna glanced down at the first question on the paper and thought as hard as she could. 'Excelsior, this is Joanna. I am going to ask you some questions and you must answer them. First question: What are you?'

Excelsior's answer exploded in her mind with such enthusiasm that she nearly fell over.

'Hi JoJo! My! Excelsior's a bit formal for a Saturday morning, why not XL – it's much cooler.'

Joanna took a deep breath to steady herself and repeated the question, this time leaving out his name. 'This is Joanna. I am going to ask you some questions and you must answer them. First question: what are you?'

'You know what I am, I'm a dragon.'

Relieved that he'd replied, Joanna quickly asked the second question, thinking it as firmly as she could.

'Question two: what is your name?'

To her surprise he answered immediately, 'My name is Excelsior.' She continued to the third question before he had any chance to add anything else.

'Question three: what type of dragon are you?'

'I'm a Silver Spiked-Back Dragon and I love my spikes, don't you? They're so sharp and pointy.'

Secretly Joanna agreed, but she was already beginning to realise what Spiky Mike was getting at, if she gave Excelsior an inch he'd take the whole mile and never shut up. She could feel his thoughts battering her mind, looking for a tiny chink or weakness.

She looked down at the piece of paper on which Spiky Mike had written the four questions. This was the one that had made her heart skip the first time she'd read it. She took a breath and thought as hard as she could. 'Question four: shall we mind-blend?'

She prepared her mind for a sudden explosion of thoughts but nothing happened. Absolute silence. She pressed her cheek more firmly against the dragon and asked him again.

'Question four: shall we mind-blend?'

There was still no reply. Joanna was just about to ask again, when it occurred to her that Excelsior might not understand what they were doing. 'Look, I'm sorry XL, I've got to ask you these questions so that I can learn to fly you. You've got to answer.'

Straight away she knew she had done the wrong thing. His response was instant and non-stop.

'Oh, who cares about questions! Just think, when you can fly we can have all sorts of adventures, excursions over the sea, scaring old ladies, chasing other dragons ...' Joanna couldn't shut him up. She jumped up and pulling her face away from Excelsior shouted aloud, 'Excelsior, shut up. I don't want to hear.' Excelsior went into an immediate sulk and fell silent. Joanna looked over to Spiky Mike expecting to get a telling off for not doing as he asked. But he simply said, 'Right, start again from the beginning and just stick to the questions.'

Joanna repeated the questions again, and this time when she asked 'Shall we mind-blend?' Excelsior answered, 'Yes!'

It was as though a door in her brain had opened. Suddenly she could *sense* Excelsior himself. With a start she realised that Excelsior must have sensed who she was too.

Afterwards Joanna didn't know how long she had sat like that even though Spiky Mike insisted it was just a few seconds.

Part Two

HOLIDAYS

Easter Holidays

Chapter 9

A Visit to Lupin Designs

First Day of the Holidays

Joanna's days quickly took on a regular pattern. Every afternoon after school she would go to the caves for one hour and repeat the four questions. Much to Joanna's relief it was usually Agnes who would meet her and take her down to Excelsior's cave to practise, after which she would go and watch Agnes turn the new dragon egg that had arrived. In fact Spiky Mike was often away for the whole week but when she asked him what else he did he snapped at her to get on with learning how to mind-blend. The questions seemed to be endlessly repetitive, but soon Joanna began to find that they had a rhythm of their own, and by the time the Easter holidays had arrived she could ask the four questions without Excelsior interrupting or commenting. In fact she was beginning to find that she didn't have to use words, somehow the ideas seemed to flow from her mind to Excelsior's and back seamlessly.

'It's like pouring water from one jug into another and back again, isn't it?' Joanna told Spiky Mike. It was the first day of the holidays and she'd just managed to run through the whole mind-blending sequence in less than a minute. She was feeling very proud of herself and anxious to make the most of her time. 'So what are we doing today?' she asked hoping he would teach her how to make a deeper mind-blend.

'Actually, Mr Marlowe would like a word with you,' replied Spiky Mike, 'he's in his study.'

Vincent's study was the one place in the caves Joanna hadn't been into and she felt very curious about it. It was obviously a special place because neither Spiky Mike nor Agnes went in unless they had been asked. Her parents had gone into the study on the first morning they had visited the caves, but when she had asked them about it all they said was that Vincent was obviously a very clever man.

She knocked firmly on the door and waited for the reply, but none came. So she knocked again, a little louder this time. There was still no reply. Joanna stood there wondering what to do, until finally her curiosity got the better of her. She opened the door. Vincent was sitting on a chair facing away from her. Joanna took a step forward. 'Excuse me Mr Marlowe, I don't think you heard me knock. It's ...' Her voice trailed off as she found herself gazing at a small fire of silver flames. Joanna felt she had interrupted something personal and private and was slowly making her way out of the room when she heard Vincent say, 'Come in my dear, I was just finishing off a little experiment that took a little longer than I had anticipated.'

'I've never seen silver fire before!' said Joanna,

'Not many people have,' replied Vincent.

'What's it for?' asked Joanna.

'It's a fire that can purify and transform.'

'Oh,' said Joanna, 'transform what?'

'Excelsior for one!' smiled Vincent. 'He was born in this flame – we're hoping it will make him extra fast. Of course we won't really know how fast until he begins to race. But that is for later. I believe it is the first day of your holidays, so instead of your lesson with Spiky Mike, we are going shopping for your flying kit. All dragon flyers must wear the appropriate clothing. Not only is it necessary for your protection, but when you're racing it is part of the regulations of the WDRF that you wear the colours appropriate to the caves you represent, which in our case are …?'

'Gold and black,' answered Joanna.

'Correct,' said Vincent. 'So get your coat, we're about to pay a visit to the very best establishment there is for the purchasing of dragon racing suits – Lupin Designs. And it just so happens that its owner, Ms Lotty Lupin, is a very dear friend of mine.'

Any further thoughts that Joanna might have had about the silver fire were forgotten as she followed Vincent out of his study. It was apparent that everyone in the Brixton Dragon Caves regarded an outing to Ms Lupin's as a treat. Both Agnes and Spiky Mike were already waiting by the lift and were in high spirits. Agnes was always smartly dressed but to Joanna's astonishment (and amusement) Spiky Mike seemed to have gelled his hair and changed into a pair of very expensive trainers.

Lupin Designs was in a small exclusive mews in the middle of Mayfair. Only minutes away from the hustle and bustle of Central London, the fashion house was renowned for designs that 'combined cosmopolitan street credibility with classic style and the practical needs of a demanding sport' or so Joanna read in the glossy magazine on the table in reception.

'Ms Lupin has been told of your arrival and sends her apologies,' explained the receptionist. 'Her previous appointment has taken much longer than expected. Can I offer you tea or coffee while you're waiting?'

They had just finished their coffee and biscuits (with freshly squeezed orange for Joanna) when the receptionist came over to tell them that Ms Lupin was now ready to see them and would they like to make their way up. Joanna was first at the lift and was about to push the button, when the lift-doors opened, and out stepped Ms Lupin's previous clients. There was a tall powerfully-built man, about her dad's age, very smartly dressed in a dark suit, next a young black man with film star good looks and very trendy clothes, and finally a young pretty black woman equally fashionably dressed. 'Perhaps they're models,' thought Joanna admiringly. They walked passed, seemingly oblivious of Joanna's existence, but stopped immediately on seeing Vincent and Spiky Mike. Joanna watched in amazement. She had never seen such dislike on so many faces all at the same time. The first man, standing in the middle of the lobby as if he owned the place, gave a mock wave of his hand and sneered. 'So Marlowe, I hear you have a new dragon, let's hope it proves a little more successful than your last one … that's if you can persuade anyone to fly it! And I'd keep a close eye on your trainer if I were you – in case he makes up all sorts of lies behind your back.'

Joanna could only listen in astonishment. 'Come on, Vincent,' she thought, 'Say something back.' And then she noticed that Vincent was trying to restrain Spiky Mike, who was ready to explode.

Fortunately Agnes stepped forward saying, 'Vincent do hurry; we mustn't keep Ms Lupin waiting.' Somehow she got the Brixton party into the lift, and the lift-doors closed separating the two parties.

'I'm sorry about that little incident,' said Vincent, turning immediately to Joanna. 'I hope it didn't upset you too much.'

'Who was that horrible man?' exclaimed Joanna.

'That was Marius King, owner of the Brighton Pavilion Caves, home of the current champion, and our greatest rivals.'

'But he was so rude to you and Spiky Mike!' said Joanna.

'We have different ideas about how things should be done,' sighed Vincent.

'We have nothing, nothing in common with that …' interrupted Spiky Mike. 'I'm just glad he was so full of himself that he didn't notice you, Joanna, and that is no bad thing. The less he knows about our plans the better. On the other hand we saw his new flyer – I recognised him, he's Hannibal Henry Oliver. His mother was a supreme champion flyer from the USA, one of the best. At least we know who we're up against.'

Joanna wanted to ask a lot more questions. She'd guessed there'd be plenty of rivalry between the different dragon caves – she'd heard her brother and parents after a football match – but she'd never have imagined there would be such bad feelings between them. Vincent was obviously quite upset and from the look of it, Spiky Mike was bothered about their choice of flyer. Hannibal Henry Oliver already looked like a champion – tall and strong and everything she wasn't … Perhaps Agnes guessed how Joanna was feeling for she suddenly took hold of Joanna's hand. 'Don't you go takin' any notice my dear. We've got a winning team, not that Marius King would recognise it if it stared him in the face. And we certainly won't let him spoil our visit to Ms Lupin.'

The lift-doors opened and Joanna gasped in surprise. The room was full of glass jars filled with sparkling jewelled rhinestones, beads and sequins. Garlands of silk flowers, fancy metal chains and rainbows of ribbons dangled from the ceiling and everywhere there were baskets filled with soft silky material. But the contents of the room were nothing compared to Ms Lupin. As soon as she stepped forward to greet them, Joanna knew that Ms Lupin was just the most beautiful person she had ever seen. Her gorgeous face shone out from long dark brown hair that flowed down her back in wave upon wave, like some dark river, reminding Joanna of a picture of wood nymphs she had seen in one of her Dad's books on paintings, except that Ms Lupin was wearing an extraordinary creation of shimmering cerise and silver that made her look like one of the models in her mum's magazines. But Ms Lupin wasn't one of those sullen models of the catwalk; lovely both in looks and person, she threw her arms open wide and kissed Vincent, Spiky Mike and then Agnes. 'So lovely to see you again, I'm so sorry you had to be kept waiting.'

Then Ms Lupin turned to Joanna and smiled. 'Vincent, please introduce us.'

Vincent gave a little formal bow to both ladies.

'Lotty, may I introduce to you our new dragon flyer, Ms Joanna Morris. Joanna, may I introduce Ms Lotty Lupin, owner and designer of Lupin Designs.' Ms Lupin kissed Joanna on both cheeks. 'Welcome to Lupin Designs. Do call me Lotty. Now come and sit down and we can get down to business.' She led them to three sofas around a low glass table that was covered in an array of fashion books and glossy magazines.

'Come and sit next to me Joanna.' Ms Lupin patted the cushion next to her on the sofa. 'So you are to be the new flyer for the Brixton Caves. Well, apart from your practice kits, which you can choose downstairs, you'll need a special kit especially for the races – and that's what I will design for you. First I want to find out what sort of things you like to wear and then we will look through these books to show you some current designs. After that I'll need to take your measurements.'

Ms Lupin picked up a tiny silk-covered notebook and a tiny pencil. 'So Joanna, tell me about the things you like to wear.'

'Well,' said Joanna, sinking into the soft silky cushioned sofa, 'my favourite colour is yellow – but I like to wear blue or black clothes best – only my mum doesn't like it when I choose too much black; and I definitely prefer wearing trousers.'

'And what about shoes?' asked Ms Lupin, noting down everything Joanna said.

'I suppose boots or trainers, but really anything that makes me look taller.'

'And your hair?' asked Ms Lupin. 'Will you be keeping it long? Many flyers prefer short hair because it's more comfortable under a helmet.'

'Oh!' said Joanna, feeling a bit shocked. 'Do I have to cut it? I really like it long and I'm used to having it tied up for school anyway.'

'Plaits would be best,' smiled Ms Lupin. 'So when you try on your helmet, plait your hair first to make sure we get the right size. Your hair is lovely and I agree it would be a shame to cut it. And finally, do you prefer zips or buttons? Buttons are quite fun, but very fiddly.'

'Zips then,' laughed Joanna.

'Next I want you to take a look at some actual designs,' said Ms Lupin picking up a large book from the table. 'Look through these and tell me if you see anything you like. This section will be most useful as these are designs for the petite shape.' Joanna read the title on the book: *High Flyers: Designs for Dragon Racing by Lotty Lupin*.

The book was divided into different sections – jackets and tops, trousers, all-in-one suits, headwear and footwear. She turned to the jacket section. As she turned the pages, models wearing jackets of every size, shape and combination of colour were arrayed before her. There were jackets with fastenings of two-way diagonal zips, safety pins and some with secret fastenings that made the jacket look like a second skin. On the back of each jacket was the name of the flyer and their cave, but perhaps most wonderful of all, on each jacket was a design of a dragon made from glittering rhinestones, sequins and beads.

'I love all of them,' Joanna exclaimed. 'How will I choose?'

'Just take your time,' said Ms Lupin. 'I'm sure one will suddenly catch your attention.' Joanna looked at page after page and then on the final page she gave a little gasp, 'Oh! I've seen this one before!' She pointed to a jacket that was tight-fitting to the waist but then flared out like a short skirt. Joanna read that it was a jacket with peplum and was quilted for extra warmth. Where had she seen it before? Suddenly she knew.

'I saw this reflected in Excelsior's eyes the first time I met him crawling down the wall of the town hall when he chose me for his flyer. That's really weird – it must be the one I'm suppose to choose.'

'Excelsior *chose* you? How unusual … and it

looks as if he's chosen your jacket too. It looks particularly good with the trousers on page 75.' But instead of turning to page 75 Ms Lupin hastily took the book off Joanna. 'Now come next door so that my assistant can measure you.' 'Can't I see the trousers?' asked Joanna, thinking Ms Lupin seemed a bit flustered.

'In a minute.'

'Have I said something wrong?' puzzled Joanna as she followed Ms Lupin into a neighbouring workroom where a young woman was stitching sequins to a wonderful leather jacket. 'Ah Stephanie,' said Ms Lupin, 'Joanna is ready to be measured.'

'Hi,' said Stephanie, taking a tape measure off the table, 'ever been measured before?'

It had never occurred to Joanna before just how many parts of her there were to be measured. She had to … stand up straight … turn round … stretch here … lift there. They still hadn't quite finished when Stephanie's phone rang.

'Excuse me, Joanna,' she smiled. 'I just need to take this call. If you don't mind I'll take it in my office next door. '

While she was waiting Joanna wandered over to a board filled with sequin designs of dragons. Suddenly through the wall came the sound of Ms Lupin's voice.

'… She's very young! Too young to involve in your own battles with Marius King! What do you think you're playing at?'

Joanna wanted to hear more but just then Stephanie came back. 'Sorry about that Joanna, now where were we? Oh yes, just a couple of head measurements and then you can go back to Ms Lupin.'

Joanna felt quite nervous as she saw Vincent sitting on the sofa. She half expected to hear him say, 'I'm sorry Joanna I've made a terrible mistake and we won't be needing your flying things.' But in fact everyone was all smiles. Vincent had obviously said enough to lessen Ms Lupin's fears.

'So Joanna, I think we're ready to look at trousers,' said Ms Lupin opening the design book at page 75. 'I really think these will suit you, and they look sensational in gold.' Immediately Joanna fell in love with them. They were tight fitting, but with a flare from the knee down, and down the outside of each leg a dragon's tail was depicted in sparkling sequins and metallic thread. 'I've just got to have these trousers,' she exclaimed, 'then I'll definitely look the part.'

Choosing the boots was a little more difficult. Spiky Mike refused to let her have any sort of heel. 'You're not at some school disco!' he snapped when Joanna pleaded with him. In the end she chose a pair of black boots that had dragon's heads on the toes.

Her helmet was streamlined and reminded Joanna of the ones she'd seen Olympic cyclists wear. As well as her official racing kit Joanna needed two practice kits. Much to her disappointment, the practice kits were all very plain; it wasn't too difficult to choose between black and black.

'And finally, one last but very important detail,' said Ms Lupin, 'what name would you like on the back of your jacket?' Immediately Joanna replied, 'JoJo – that's what Excelsior calls me.'

'Does he now!' smiled Ms Lupin. 'Then JoJo it shall be.'

That night Joanna lay awake in bed thinking about everything she had heard and seen that day. 'I suppose I've been so busy learning to mind-blend with Excelsior I've never really thought about the rest of the dragon racing world. Perhaps it's time I found out – especially about Marius King! There's bound to be something in those dragon magazines Vincent lent to Dad.' Joanna crept carefully into her parents' room to get them. Back in her room she turned on her bedroom light and started to flick through the most recent edition. 'But it's all about Marius King. He's won everything!' She picked up an older magazine. Marius King was staring up at her again but there was someone else in the photograph that made her gasp in surprise. 'That's Spiky Mike! And there he is again!' In fact Spiky Mike was in just about every magazine and always with the winner of a race. Joanna had vaguely taken in that he was a successful trainer, but it began to dawn on her just how good he was. Then at the bottom of an article came another surprise. A photo of Spiky Mike standing with his arm around a young woman. 'She's the one I saw this morning!'

Joanna read *'Dream Team – Spiky Mike and his new assistant, Afra Power, join Marius King at the Brighton Pavilion Caves. A bright and rosy future lie ahead for this young couple whose names, rumour says, are linked romantically as well as professionally.'* Absolutely fascinated, Joanna scoured other magazines for more. What she found was headline news – *Spiky Mike Quits Dragon Lord Supremo.* Joanna looked at the date on the magazine. 'October? – only six months ago! But it doesn't say anything about why he left. I wonder if the November magazine will tell me anything?' But by November, Spiky Mike had disappeared completely from the pages.

Chapter 10

A Visit to the Park

Last Day of the Holidays

Over the next few days Joanna discovered one further thing about Spiky Mike – that as far as he was concerned the school holidays meant mind-blending, mind-blending and more mind-blending. 'We need to really get ahead of ourselves before you go back to school,' he insisted. 'Now Hannibal Henry Oliver ...'

'Now Hannibal Henry Oliver ...' mimicked Joanna to herself as she settled down besides Excelsior.

'Did you say something, Joanna?' snapped Spiky Mike.

'Me?' Joanna replied innocently. 'I was just getting ready to mind-blend.'

'And *why* do you need to practise mind-blending, Joanna?'

'Because that's how you fly a dragon?'

'Exactly!' said Spiky Mike, 'and, *if* you do as you are told, then by the end of the holidays *you* will be ready for Excelsior's first flight.'

'WHAT!' Joanna looked up at Spiky Mike in astonishment. 'Excelsior fly? Outside? In the sky? When?'

'Last day of the holidays.' He smiled unexpectedly.

'And what will *I* do?' she asked excitedly.

'Mind-blend!' groaned Spiky Mike, in exasperation. 'What else!'

Excelsior was only told about the flight the afternoon before. He was overjoyed at the thought of flying outside. 'Where are we going? Somewhere exciting?'

'Just the local park,' said Joanna. 'According to Agnes, Vincent has arranged for us to use the park every morning before it's opened to anyone else.'

'A whole park just for us? I can't wait! JoJo, it seems all my plans for tomorrow have been changed in an instant, so do me a favour and tell

Spiky Mike that I'm going to have a little sleep
– I'll need to be at my best tomorrow.'

To Joanna's amusement Excelsior lay down on
the floor of his cave, closed his eyes and started to
snore. Spiky Mike gave a snort of disgust. 'That
dragon! Oh well Joanna, you should probably do
the same, it's going to be an early start tomorrow.
Tell your mum I'll pick you up at 5.30 tomorrow
morning.'

The morning did not start well for Joanna. She
stormed into the kitchen where her mother, still
in her dressing gown, was drinking a cup of tea.
'Who said Aaron could come?'

'Joanna, stop shouting!' said her mother.

'Actually, Vincent said I could come!' said
Aaron, following his sister into the kitchen. 'Tell
her, Mum. He said to see a dragon fly for the first
time was something everyone should experience.'

'Be quiet the pair of you! If you wake your
father with all that shouting neither of you will
be going.'

'When?' asked Joanna, feeling annoyed that
Aaron should actually have Vincent on his side.

'He phoned yesterday evening, when you were
in the bath,' replied her mother. 'I really didn't
think you'd mind – in fact I thought you might
enjoy having someone to share it with.' 'Oh!' said

Joanna sheepishly, 'I hadn't thought of that. Hey Aaron, won't it be funny being in the park before anyone else?'

'Never mind the chatter,' interrupted her mum. 'You both need to get a move on; Spiky Mike will be here soon.'

At 5.30 exactly Spiky Mike arrived to pick up the children. They climbed into the van and set off for the nearby park. As they drove along Joanna noticed that Excelsior was strangely quiet in the back of the van. Gently she called his name, but found to her surprise that he was fast asleep. 'Wake up, Lazy!' she laughed. 'Look, we're driving through the park gates.' Excelsior seemed to give a snort of disgust and drowsily replied, 'I'm not too keen on early mornings! A dragon needs his beauty sleep you know!'

Spiky Mike caught sight of the still snoozing dragon and snapped, 'They're all the same – hate getting up early. Oi! Excelsior! Wakey, wakey! Time to get your wings flapping!' He parked the van under the trees and Joanna and Aaron jumped out quickly, eager to start. Together they opened the van doors, but Excelsior did not move an inch. Spiky Mike slid out a long pole and gave the dragon a prod. 'Time to get going, Excelsior!' Still Excelsior would not budge. Joanna tried to call him, but felt as if she had met a brick wall. 'He won't answer me at all,' called Joanna; she felt quite shocked.

'Don't worry,' replied Spiky Mike. 'Dragons hate early starts – but they have to learn, like the rest of us, that sometimes these things are not a matter of choice.' He prodded Excelsior again with the pole, only this time Joanna noticed one end had a loop of rope attached to it. When Excelsior still refused to move, Spiky Mike slid the rope over his tail and gave a quick flick. Instantly Excelsior jumped up and was out of the van. Aaron was very impressed. 'Wow that was great! Could you teach me how to do that?'

Joanna looked quite shocked. 'Didn't it hurt?'

'No,' grinned Spiky Mike, 'but it works every time.' Joanna was relieved to see that Excelsior was not only fine, but was back to his usual perky self. He walked slowly over to a wide-open piece of grass and started to arch his neck. Joanna could see his wings were trembling and then with a sudden loud roar of delight that startled Joanna – and all the birds in the nearby trees – he leapt up into the air. The dragon's wings sprang out from his side and started to beat the air with strong wild strokes so that he soared up into the sky. There was no need to do anything but watch and they gazed up into the sky, lost in the delights of watching a dragon find his wings. Excelsior's sleek, silver body would twist and flick with the changing currents of air or dive in a series of swoops till he was just above their heads, then with a beat of his wings he would soar skyward again. Spiky Mike came over to where Joanna was watching. 'You've spent your holidays practising – and now it's time to find out why. Go on; ask the mind-blending questions.'

Silently, Joanna started to repeat them to herself then suddenly it was as though she too were soaring up to the heavens. The shock of it jolted her mind back into her own body and she felt her feet back on the ground – but suddenly she knew, she knew what it would *be* like, *feel* like, to fly on a dragon … it was the best, the only thing and soon, soon it would happen for real. Spiky Mike grinned at her. 'Magic, eh? Well done.'

She stared up again at Excelsior and smiled and at that moment the sun escaped from the early morning cloud and poured its golden rays on to the dragon so that he shone with a silver luminous light.

'Even after all these years there is nothing as beautiful as a dragon in flight,' said a voice. Vincent was standing behind her. She had been so absorbed in watching Excelsior that she hadn't noticed his arrival. Spiky Mike however, already wanted to discuss technicalities with Vincent. 'Excelsior's got good balance and a natural elasticity in his spine, but we're going to have to watch for over-beat in the downward sweep of wing. It's a common fault in the Silver Spiked-Back and it loses valuable time in a race. I'd better set up a series of exercises to correct that before it becomes too much of a habit.' Vincent nodded in agreement. Joanna tried to see what they were talking about. 'I can't see anything wrong at all. In fact I think he looks just perfect.'

'All right, Joanna,' called Spiky Mike, 'call Excelsior in.'

Joanna watched the dragon twist and turn one more time before she called out to him, 'Hey XL, it's time to land.'

'Wheeeeeee! Watch me flyyyyyyyyy!' shouted Excelsior. 'Isn't this the best!'

'Oh yes! Did you feel me before, when I felt myself rise with you?' 'But of course!' replied Excelsior, 'why did you let go so quickly? Shall I do a loop-the-loop again?'

'I'd love you to,' said Joanna, 'but XL, Spiky Mike says its time to come back down!'

'He's such a spoilsport!' Excelsior slowly started to circle round them as he began to descend. He was just about to land, when something caught his attention. Joanna said afterwards that Excelsior just stopped in mid-air and then went careering off down the hill.

'What the ...' Spiky Mike turned angrily towards Joanna. 'Tell that crazy dragon to get back here immediately.' Joanna began calling out to Excelsior, but the only reply was, 'Can't stop or it'll be too late. Get everyone to come and help.'

Joanna turned back to the others. 'Help! Quick! Someone needs help!' Everyone started to run down the hill to where Excelsior was circling around the top of a great oak tree. What was he doing? Spiky Mike reached the tree first and began to climb up into the branches. But he didn't get very far before he started to climb down again. What was going on?

Joanna called again to Excelsior, 'XL, what's happening?' but all he answered was, 'Don't worry, I can get him.' Joanna suddenly caught a glimpse of a waving hand at the top of the tree. Excelsior disappeared into the branches and she caught brief flashes of his silver body hidden amongst the leaves. A few seconds later Excelsior flew back out of the treetop. Joanna gasped, 'There's somebody on XL's back!' Immediately Joanna knew who it was – and she felt as if someone had punched her in the stomach – it was Aaron! She couldn't bear to watch. She started to run. Away – just away from *him,* her own brother! *He* was flying on *her* dragon! How could he! How could Excelsior have let him? In the end she threw herself down to the ground under a huge tree. She had a stitch in her side and there were tears running down her cheeks, but she ignored these, unable to think of anything other than what she had seen. Her own brother had flown on Excelsior!

Vincent eventually found her still sitting under the tree. He stood there for a moment looking down at her, not saying a word and Joanna realised with a shock that he was upset. 'What on earth did you run off like that for? I've just spent the last hour searching for you.'

Joanna looked up at him. 'I hate my brother! He always spoils everything. Dragon racing is mine!'

Vincent gave a little smile. 'Oh I see, a small dose of sibling rivalry.'

'It's not a small dose of anything,' snapped Joanna, 'Aaron flew on Excelsior! He's my dragon – it should have been me!'

'Actually Excelsior only "carried" your brother on his back – not at all the same thing as "flying" a dragon. Your brother has been very silly and he's as upset as you are about the whole thing.

The important thing to remember though is that nobody is hurt. There could have been a very nasty accident.'

'But why was Aaron in the tree anyway?' asked Joanna, 'I've never seen him climb a tree before.'

'He said he wanted a better view ... and Joanna, you're not the only one to feel jealous. Has it ever occurred to you that Aaron might like to be a dragon flyer too?'

Joanna looked up and saw Aaron just a little way off, sitting under another tree. She could hardly believe he could be jealous of her. She was so used to it being the other way round. Funny she'd always thought it would make her feel good to be better at something than her brother; but it didn't – perhaps because she understood too well how horrible he would be feeling. He gave her a wave and she waved back. He walked slowly over. 'Jo, I'm sorry; I didn't mean to get stuck in the tree. I hope Excelsior's all right. Spiky Mike said ...'

'What's the matter with Excelsior?' interrupted Joanna alarmed. 'He is all right, isn't he?'

'Calm down, Joanna,' replied Vincent. 'It's nothing to worry about. Just a bit of wing-strain – at worst he'll need a few days rest. As for the tree – Perhaps I should write a letter of apology to the park authorities!'

Chapter 11

Water and Fire

Marius King put down the telephone and smiled across the desk at Afra and Hannibal. 'Well, that's confirmed. Madame Akua herself will be leading a party of representatives from the WDRF to see Prometheus' first flight. There are still those in the Federation who are questioning the breeding of a Jewel Dragon for racing. But if it's seen that Madame Akua has given her endorsement to the project nobody will be able to stop us. Our guests will arrive in Brighton tomorrow morning but will go straight to the flight area itself. After the flight we'll return to the caves for lunch. Should be a good day.'

'Hey, Madam Akua, she's President of the

WDRF this year, isn't she!' remarked Hannibal. 'I remember goin' with Mom to watch her at the speed trials in San Francisco the year she became Supreme Champion – I must have been about five.'

Afra glanced over at Hannibal. He'd grown up surrounded by the world of dragon racing ... just like someone else she knew! Did they know how fortunate they were? Her own family were always asking when was she going to get a *proper* job. She was certainly looking forward to meeting Madame Akua tomorrow and she was determined to impress her. She stood up. 'Marius, I would just like to take Hannibal through his mind-blending exercises before tomorrow.' Marius dismissed them with a wave of his hand and turned back to his computer screen.

Afra followed Hannibal down the passageway. She was feeling extremely pleased with his progress. Hannibal was so cool and confident; it seemed that the primary stages of mind-blending with Prometheus had been no effort at all. He was of course impatient to progress to the deeper levels of mind-blending. As for Prometheus, she had been surprised to find him so co-operative a dragon. Everything was going according to plan – so why did she still have misgivings about it all?

Prometheus was lying in his cave. A deep split in the rock had been carefully carved out for him. He was longer and sleeker than most Jewel Dragons his age, or so it seemed to Afra. The large wings that had been present at his birth were carefully folded against his body and it was obvious to everyone that he was going to be extremely fast.

'Hannibal, I'm sure like me you really want to impress our guests tomorrow. As it's a "first flight" they're going to expect to see you control Prometheus' landing. So let's just go through the command sequence.'

'What! Again! I can do that standing on my head. Why not really impress them and show them a deeper mind-blend – I can feel Prometheus calling me!'

Afra frowned, 'It's not that I want to stop you, but you know how disorientating they can be at first – it's the sort of thing you need to practise on your own.'

'Look, I'm ready, so let's do it,' Hannibal replied.

Hannibal walked over to Prometheus – the dragon's eyes were almost closed so that it appeared to be asleep, but Hannibal knew better and pressed his own face firmly against that of the dragon. He looked over at Afra and said, 'What next?'

'Hannibal, I don't think this is good idea. If we go too fast too quickly you might aggravate Prometheus.'

He turned back to face her. 'I thought you wanted to impress Madame Akua …'

'Oh very well, but you must break it when I tell you and don't go too deep. Don't synchronise unless I tell you!'

Afra stood back and watched Hannibal's dark face tense in concentration and then as he started to mind-blend she saw his face muscles relax. Unless she stopped him now he would synchronise with the dragon automatically. Should she let him? Afra felt herself hold her breath as slowly Hannibal's facial movements began to synchronise with those of the dragon. She barely waited a minute before she said, 'Hannibal, break the mind-blend. Ask him the routine questions.'

Reluctantly Hannibal began to break the mind-blend. 'Dragon Prometheus – this is H_20 …' until finally he pulled his head away from the dragon. 'Hey – why did you make me break contact so quickly – it was like we were just one creature working together? And his mind! – he let me in and it was like pure power – only I was in control. Come on, let's do it again!'

'No, that's enough Hannibal; it's vital that the

WDRF see you in complete control tomorrow. If they don't endorse our application then we won't be able to race Prometheus. Just think, in a few months not only will you be mind-blending with Prometheus but you'll be flying him too.'

The Brighton Caves owned a large estate on the South Downs overlooking the sea. Here dragon flying could take place away from prying eyes. The next morning, a party of about ten people made their way to a small stand on the cliff top. Marius King strode confidently forward to greet his guests. 'Good morning Madame Akua, I trust you had a good journey.'

'Good morning Mr King, we are delighted to be here. My colleagues and I are following your work with interest. The papers Dr Alexander sent proved very valuable background reading and of course I am thrilled that your new flyer is Hannibal Oliver. His mother is a great friend of mine.'

'And there is the young man in question,' said Marius King with a smile, pointing over towards the area where Hannibal was deep in conversation with Afra. At a signal from Afra, Marius King turned to his guests, 'Now ladies and gentlemen let's make our way to our seats.'

Marius King accompanied Madame Akua to her seat, where Dr Alexander was on hand to answer any of her questions. He was already deep in conversation with the WDRF veterinary surgeon, Dr Adam Mundy and the WDRF Dragon Welfare Officer Tatiana Burnofski. On seeing Dr Mundy, Marius King interrupted their conversation. 'Adam, good to see you after all this time.' Marius King turned back to Madame Akua, 'Dr Mundy and I were at university together. It was Adam who introduced me to the world of dragon racing. Well Adam, I think you'll be very interested in the progress Dr Alexander is making with the problem of dragon obesity.' All further conversation stopped as a voice on a tannoy announced the beginning of the flight. Everyone settled down in their seat and watched as the door of a large transporter van on the edge of the field slid noiselessly up. At first all anyone could see was the darkness of the inside of the van, then suddenly an emerald flash of dragon shot out into the sky. Prometheus' rainbow coloured underbelly, unique to Jewel Dragons, shimmered and sparkled in the golden rays of sun. Then slowly Prometheus stretched out his great wings like two wonderful enormous silken fans and glided effortlessly across the sky sending ripples of excitement and admiration through the guests. 'Look at those wings,' Dr Mundy exclaimed. 'I've never seen anything like it!'

But the beauty of the dragon was as nothing to its speed and power. With just a few beats of its magnificent wings the dragon picked up speed and tore across the sky like a streak of green lightning. Then with a whip of his great spiked tail Prometheus twisted and turned and changed direction. Was such agility possible? It was evident to all that here was a dragon like nothing they had seen before. Could such a dragon be controlled? At a signal from Afra, Hannibal stepped forward so that he was standing immediately in front of the spectators and began to order the dragon to land. Prometheus descended rapidly in a spiralling flight and landed a few feet away from Hannibal, closing its great wings against its body. It was a precision landing straight from the textbook and Marius King saw Madame Akua nodding in approval. 'It's like watching his mother all over again. Perfect control.'

The successful flight was followed by an equally successful lunch at the end of which Madame Akua herself personally signed the licence and registration papers that permitted the Brighton Pavilion Caves to race the Jewel Dragon. 'Well Marius, it's been a truly memorable day. Hannibal's control of the dragon is remarkable.' Madame Akua looked around the room for Hannibal, but he was nowhere too be seen. 'Our young friend seems to have disappeared. Never mind! Afra, I'm sure you'll pass on my congratulations. I congratulate you too – I'm pleased to see that you are really beginning to come into your own as a trainer.' Afra felt like bursting with pride. 'It's been such a privilege working as part of such a team. I can't wait to see Prometheus and Hannibal in their first race!'

Hannibal had slipped quickly and quietly out of the lunch party. What did he want with social chitchat when that very morning he had heard the dragon call to him? He had not been able to answer then but he would now.

The cave was dark when Hannibal entered but he left it that way. Prometheus didn't like light spoiling his darkness. Kneeling down he pressed his face against the dragon's. There was no need to ask the questions. He was there with Prometheus, feeling the fire in his belly ... remembering the thrill of flight and most of all sensing the power of the dragon's mind calling to his own. Nothing else mattered now. Slowly at first and then suddenly faster, not wanting to hold back, he let his mind open up fully to the power of the dragon. Terrible, but wonderful! Water, meeting Fire.

Chapter 12

Mouse

Summer Holidays

The early morning sessions quickly became a regular feature of Joanna's life and what with school work as well she was relieved when the summer holidays arrived. The amazing thing was that despite all the early hours and the long training sessions Joanna's school work had improved tremendously. Her end of year report was positively glowing with praise. Out of school, Joanna's relationship with Spiky Mike was not going well.

'I'm not surprised everyone calls him "Spiky" Mike,' grumbled Joanna to Agnes after a particularly trying session. 'NOTHING I do is ever good enough for him!'

'Perhaps now it's the holidays things will be easier; although you coped marvellously with training and school,' Agnes replied diplomatically. 'When do you start your flying course? I hear Spiky Mike has arranged for you to go up to a centre in Wales.'

'Next Saturday' said Joanna. 'And guess what? Spiky Mike's not there for the first two weeks! Hurray!'

Joanna was very excited about her trip to Wales.

'The centre is run by some very good friends of mine,' said Spiky Mike. 'It's set right up in the mountains of Snowdonia; you'll have a wonderful time!'

'What will I actually do there?' asked Joanna

'Why, you'll learn how to fly of course.'

'Isn't that what I've been learning all along?' replied Joanna.

'So far you've learnt about mind-blending, now you're going to learn how to sit on a dragon's back and stay on as it flies. The dragons at the centre are all ideal; they are much bigger and slower than racing dragons and very easy to control.'

'But what about Excelsior?'

'I will drive up with Excelsior for the second two weeks.'

'And will I get to fly Excelsior? I mean in the sky?' asked Joanna excitedly. 'Of course, what else would you do, silly girl?' retorted Spiky Mike, but Joanna could see that he was really as thrilled as she was.

Excelsior was equally excited when she came to say goodbye – she thought he might have been jealous at the thought of her flying other dragons. 'Oh Wales, there'll be misty mountains full of ancient dragon caves and by the time I get there perhaps you'll have found some forgotten, long lost treasure. As for other dragons – don't expect them to be as handsome as me. Some of them have terribly fat stomachs you know and have to go on diets and fly extra long distances to tone up their muscles. I'm quite looking forward to tearing up a few mountains myself before breakfast.'

'Really,' said Joanna, 'I'll believe that when I see it!'

It was agreed that Joanna's parents would take Joanna to Wales, having dropped Aaron off at his football summer camp on the way. Then they would go for a holiday of their own somewhere on the coast.

The journey took the best part of the day and

despite the usual family squabbles Joanna couldn't help but enjoy it. As the car radio announced five o'clock they found themselves driving up a small winding road. On one side was the greyness of the mountains climbing up into the mists, while on the other the ground fell steeply away to a thundering white-foamed river. For the past half-hour they had been looking for the sign that would direct them to the Snowdonia National Park Dragon Sanctuary. 'We must be close now. Are you sure you didn't take the wrong turning back there, Hilary?' asked Anthony Morris, peering again at the map open on his knee.

'No, I did not!' replied Joanna's mother, adding triumphantly, 'Here we are!' and she turned the car into a small lane. Joanna just glimpsed two stone gateposts carved in the shape of two great dragons. The lane seemed to go on forever through a dark tunnel of trees and then suddenly there was a large pebble-dashed house with a great slate roof, surrounded by masses of blue hydrangea bushes all in flower. However, there was no sign of a dragon.

'Come on, Joanna, don't just sit there daydreaming, come and help carry your stuff in. Remember your father and I have still got at least an hour's drive ahead of us,' said her mother. They were half-way through unpacking the car when the front door opened and down the steps came a tiny lady with a tumble of dark curls who smiled an enormous red-lipstick smile. 'Welcome! I am Lucia Balivo, owner of the Snowdonia National Park Dragon Sanctuary along with my husband, Giovanni.' She threw her arms around Joanna and gave her such an enormous hug that Joanna was left gasping for breath, 'and you must be Joanna, the bambina herself. I have heard so much about you!' Still holding Joanna tightly, she turned to Anthony and Hilary Morris. 'Let's go in. You must be exhausted after your drive.' One quick cup of tea was all Joanna's parents would allow themselves. 'We've a good hour's drive ahead of us yet, so if you don't mind we'll be off,' announced Anthony Morris. 'Please give our regards to Mr Balivo.'

'He'll be sorry to have missed you,' smiled Lucia. 'One of the dragons must be needing some extra attention otherwise he would have been back by now.'

Joanna felt herself tingle all over at the thought of the dragons. She let herself feel distracted by them as she walked back to the car with her parents. She always hated goodbyes and suddenly hoped she wouldn't be homesick. 'Now dress-up warm and eat well,' said Hilary Morris as she kissed her daughter goodbye, 'and don't forget ...'

'Hilary, COME ON!' snapped her husband, pushing her in to the car. 'She'll be just fine. Won't you, Joanna?' Joanna nodded even though she felt an enormous lump in her throat. Funny how that always happened when her parents left her anywhere, at home she couldn't wait to be on her own.

Joanna watched her parents' car disappear and turned to follow Lucia back into the house. Lucia showed her up to her room so that she could unpack. But as Lucia opened the door, Joanna was surprised to see that there was already someone else there. A girl was sitting on one of the room's two beds, reading a dragon-racing magazine. Lucia smiled at Joanna's face. 'I have not only one bambina to stay this holiday, but two, and I thought you would prefer to share. I'll leave you to introduce yourselves.' Lucia shut the door behind her and left the two girls staring at each other. But as soon as Joanna heard the other girl say, 'Hello, my name's Mouse, what's yours?' she knew they were going to be the very best of friends. By the time Lucia knocked on the door to announce that it was suppertime Joanna had discovered that Mouse (so called because she was the smallest in the family – her real name was Marcia Chatfield) came from an old dragon racing family; her parents owned the Blackpool Tower Dragon Caves and she had four older sisters who were either successful flyers or trainers – 'Which leaves me! Literally! Everyone is always forgetting me. Do you realise the rest of my family left yesterday morning to go trekking through the Himalayas – they've heard about a super rare dragon egg and as Dad's a bit of a collector of rare dragon breeds he's very anxious to get hold of it so that he can hatch it out properly. They forgot about me when it came to booking flights and by the time someone noticed, it was too late, as the plane was full. So my mum rang Lucia – she's my godmother – and arranged for me to stay here all summer.' Joanna slipped her arm through her new friend's as they made their way down the stairs. 'I can't imagine *how* they forgot you, but I'm glad they did!'

Giovanni had returned from feeding the dragons. He was small and dark like his wife, but very round; the cause of which soon became evident – dinner was amazing. As well as huge plates of pasta covered in a thick bolognaise sauce, there were cheeses and breads and mountains of salad – and for pudding, wonderful homemade tiramisu. Joanna wondered if, by the time Excelsior arrived, his wing muscles would have developed enough to carry all the extra weight she would have put on.

'So Joanna, Croeso i Cymru – Welcome to Wales!' smiled Giovanni. Joanna was quite surprised to hear him speak with a strong Welsh accent.

'Oh, I've lived up in these mountains all my life, but my grandfather was Italian and I am named after him!'

Over dinner there was plenty of conversation. 'What sort of dragons do you keep here?' asked Joanna. 'We keep three Beddgelert Riders,' said Lucia, 'they're traditional Welsh Red dragons, although not the racing variety; then there are two old Snowdonian Greens – but they don't leave their caves anymore, as they're over two hundred years old. They are royal dragons that used to live at Harlech Castle, just down the coast. We let them use two of the caves up on the mountain for a nominal rent. We have three caves for visiting dragons and we keep a couple of caves for use in an emergency.'

'Perhaps you can help me choose one of the caves for Excelsior before he arrives,' said Giovanni. 'He's a Silver Spiked-Back, isn't he?'

'Yes,' smiled Joanna.

'Silver Spiked-Back! Oh, I love those, they're such fun,' said Mouse. 'Will we be learning on the Beddgelert Riders?'

'Of course,' said Giovanni, 'just like your sisters before you. Now your lesson is at 8.30 tomorrow morning and as tomorrow will be a very busy day, I suggest an early bed.'

Up in their room, Joanna and Mouse were too excited to go to sleep so they lay awake talking. Joanna told Mouse how she had met Excelsior.

'It's like something out of a book,' laughed Mouse. 'And is Spiky Mike really your trainer?' She sounded very impressed. 'You do know he IS the best! At least, my dad always says he is. They were going to ask him to come to the Blackpool Caves but then he got the job at Brixton.'

'Agnes, our egg turner told me that Spiky Mike came to the Brixton Caves because of Excelsior,' said Joanna. 'He's supposed to be a special dragon but then I've never seen another dragon so I don't really know. I can't wait to fly him. What's it like?'

'What, flying? I don't know,' said Mouse. 'Tomorrow will be my first time too.' Joanna looked at her friend incredulously. 'But you said your parents own dragon caves. I would have thought you grew up flying dragons.' 'Grown up with them, yes,' replied Mouse, 'but it's like I said, everyone always forgets about me and so I've never learnt how to actually fly one. I haven't minded until now, but ...' Mouse was silent for a moment then suddenly she said, 'If I tell you my secret will you promise not to tell a soul ... I want to be a dragon rider acrobat.'

Joanna listened in astonishment. 'Can you do that sort of thing?'

'I don't see why not. I grew up watching the acrobats and the trapeze artists at the Blackpool Tower Circus. Last year I persuaded them to teach me and then I thought, wouldn't it be great to perform the routines on a dragon. I want to get really good and then just sort of announce it to everyone – of course I'll have to find a dragon that will let me.'

Joanna laughed, thinking that Excelsior for one would be quite happy to give it a try. 'I think it's brilliant.'

'We'll both be brilliant!' Mouse talked on, making plans for world domination but try as she could Joanna soon lost track and slipped into sleep.

Chapter 13

Earth and Air

Joanna woke next morning to find golden sunshine flooding through the curtains. Mouse was still fast asleep, so she crept quietly over to the window. The mists had lifted off the mountains, revealing all their craggy splendour. Half-way up Joanna could see a series of dark openings in the mountainside – dragon caves. A small tractor pulling a trailer was making its way up the steep track towards them. Giovanni must be going to feed the dragons.

Mouse woke up with a groan, 'Oh, do we have to get up yet?' Joanna glanced down at her watch and gave a start, 'Yes we do! It's nearly eight o'clock! Our lesson's at 8.30.'

At 8.30 sharp Giovanni arrived in his tractor,

this time pulling a trailer with seats, 'Up you get girls.' They scrambled aboard and they set off up the mountain track. A few minutes later the tractor stopped in a small green field and Joanna's heart began to thump wildly in her chest. In the middle of the field were three very large red dragons!

Giovanni jumped down from the tractor. 'There have been dragons born and bred in these mountains for centuries; this is their natural habitat. Respect them and their surroundings and they will respect you. This breed, the Beddgelert Rider, is a large slow-flying dragon; it is very tolerant, requiring only a minimum of mind-blending for a flyer to control it – not like racing dragons.' Giovanni looked over at Joanna and smiled. 'First we will learn how to greet our dragons, to mount and to dismount.'

To her relief Joanna found the morning quite straightforward. Her dragon went by the pet name of Nia. It had a much longer Welsh name of which Nia was only the first part.

'Now that you're all on first name terms,' continued Giovanni, 'ask your dragon to lower its head.' The girls followed the instructions and sure enough the dragons lowered their heads. 'Now feel at the base of its neck where the backbone meets the shoulder blades. Can you feel that hollow? That's where you sit.'

Joanna climbed up onto Nia's back with ease. Somehow she'd thought it would be a lot more difficult – like the time she'd scrabbled up onto a horse's back. The hollow was really comfortable, almost padded. 'Now lean forward and rest your head on the dragon's neck, as near to its face as you can.' Joanna leant forward. She knew from mind-blending with Excelsior what she would feel. Immediately Nia's thoughts were louder and clearer, like tuning in a radio or listening to music through headphones. She looked round at Mouse, who smiled back.

They spent the first half of the morning getting on and off until Joanna felt she could do it in her sleep, then finally Giovanni decided they were ready to start flying.

The girls climbed on to the dragons and waited for Giovanni's instructions,

'When I say, lean forward and mind-blend with your dragon. You only need to use simple words – "fly", "higher", "lower" and "land". Fly to the end of the field and land there. Right Mouse, you're first.' Joanna watched in silence as Mouse leant her face against the dragon. Immediately the dragon spread its wings and began to fly slowly down the field. Compared to Excelsior, the dragon looked as though it was flying in slow motion!

Mouse seemed to find it quite easy and waved excitedly back at Joanna

'Right, Joanna you're next,' said Giovanni. 'This is it!' thought Joanna, 'my first dragon flight.' She knew she was excited, but as she leant forward and felt Nia's warm scales against her cheek she found herself wishing it were Excelsior. A pair of fiery eyes suddenly flashed though her mind momentarily distracting her. 'Fly!' thought Joanna and her dragon launched itself upwards. Joanna felt a sudden rush of air, but not up, she was falling off! Luckily the ground was soft, but she landed with a great thud and a very red face! Mouse, full of concern for her friend, came tearing across the field whilst Giovanni just roared with laughter. 'I wondered if that would happen.'

Joanna sat there mortified – she had fallen off! It was so embarrassing. In a terrible moment of panic she found herself thinking, 'Oh no, I can't do it!'

Giovanni smiled, but stopped laughing. 'Don't worry; it's actually a good thing. Tell me, were you thinking about Excelsior?'

'Yes – I saw his eyes!' replied Joanna. 'How did you know? And why is it good? If I can't fly without falling off, I'm not going to get very far.'

'It just means that the relationship between

you and Excelsior is strong. Dragons are very good at playing mind games – it was Excelsior's way of telling you not to forget him. You'll be fine next time.' Joanna nodded; she remembered how jealous she'd felt when her brother had flown on Excelsior. So Excelsior *had* minded her coming to Wales without him! Feeling much better Joanna climbed onto Nia's back; as she did, she was sure Nia winked at her. This time, as she whispered 'fly' she felt the rush of air carry her up higher and higher – she was flying! There was Mouse down below, looking as small as her name; beyond that she could see Lucia hanging out the washing, then there was the road and far away she could even see the sea. All around her was nothing but sunshine, blue sky and the slow steady beat of dragon wings through the air and then suddenly she was at the bottom of the field. It had only taken a few seconds and she was back down on the solid greenness of the field. Mouse came running over. 'Wow, isn't it the best!' Joanna smiled at her friend, but didn't climb down immediately. Now that she had landed she could feel her heart pounding in her chest and her legs felt like they'd turned to jelly. Flying a dragon was wonderful – the most wonderful thing she'd ever done, but she knew Nia wasn't Excelsior. Suddenly, she wanted more than anything to see him. 'Soon, XL it will be us,' she thought.

Giovanni made the girls spend the next few days endlessly flying up and down the field, round and round the field, even zigzagging across the field until they were sick of seeing that small patch of green. They pleaded with him to let them fly further afield, but he just laughed at them saying, 'Practice makes perfect.'

By the end of the first week, their hard work was beginning to pay off and as their confidence grew so did their competitive spirit. Who could take off the fastest or get the highest in ten seconds? Then late on the Friday afternoon Lucia came out to watch. 'Bravo!' she cried, 'I have been watching from the window.' She turned to her husband, 'So Giovanni, how about making it really interesting – how about a race?'

Giovanni stood for a moment looking at the two girls who could hardly contain their excitement. 'Well Lucia, not much fun, a two dragon race – so I'd better race too … and if one of them can beat me, then I promise that tomorrow I'll take them both for a trek up the mountain … of course if I win …' Joanna and Mouse both stopped in their tracks. 'Oh please don't say more field,' groaned Joanna.

'Actually it was the washing-up I had in mind!'

As the three flyers settled down on to their dragons Joanna looked over at Mouse and Giovanni. She thought she could easily beat Mouse, but Giovanni? Oh, she so wanted to beat Giovanni!

'OK,' called Lucia, 'one … two … three … go!' Joanna urged Nia into the air with such ferocity that Joanna took off almost vertically; immediately she glanced around to see where Mouse and Giovanni were. Mouse was only just taking off, but Giovanni was already racing down the field. He was flying quite low, only just above the ground. 'Of course,' thought Joanna, 'why waste time and energy gaining height for such a short race.' Instinctively Joanna chased after him. Her dive was so sharp that Giovanni was immediately forced to fly up higher. Urging Nia to fly even faster, Joanna held her position right to the end of the field and landed her dragon perfectly. First! She was first! But her feeling of triumph suddenly disappeared as Giovanni landed beside her and said in a low voice, 'Where on earth did you learn that?'

Joanna hardly dared look at him; forcing someone else out of the way obviously wasn't the done thing.

'I'm sorry!' she cried, 'I won't do it again?'

'I sincerely hope you will!' interrupted Giovanni. 'It's moves like that that win races!'

'But,' said Joanna, managing at last to look Giovanni in the eye, 'you don't mind then? It's just that you seemed so shocked!'

'Only because I wasn't expecting it. Obviously mind-blending with Excelsior has already sharpened your reactions and given you an appetite for winning.'

'So do we get to fly up the mountain as you promised?' asked Joanna.

'Of course,' grinned Giovanni, 'I would have taken you anyway, but, well, Lucia and I wondered what a bit of competition would do.'

'And now you know!' said Mouse, not at all put out at coming in last.

That flight up the mountain was the first of many. It was a wild, wonderful place of high grey craggy rocks, cascading waterfalls and hidden green valleys. Joanna loved flying up there. Nia had grown up on the mountain and knew all its high twisting tracks and paths, all the overhanging outcrops of rock and the hidden pool that lay just below the summit. One afternoon the pair of them sat side by side at the edge of the water. They were alone. Mouse had stayed down below in the field to see if she could persuade her dragon, Carys, to let her try some simple acrobatics. Joanna's cheek was resting against Nia's face and an easy flow of thoughts was drifting between the two. Thoughts tinged with sadness. It was their last ride together before Excelsior arrived that evening. Both of them knew that Excelsior would not tolerate Joanna flying on Nia's back if he was around. Joanna would miss Nia. At first Joanna had felt frustrated that Nia's mind was slow compared to Excelsior. But that slowness had given Joanna the chance to learn and to appreciate the beauty of flying.

'Thank you Nia', said Joanna, 'not just for teaching me to fly, but for sharing your love of the mountains. I know I love them so much because I saw them through your thoughts.'

'Not many flyers are so careful of my thoughts,' replied Nia, 'and I should know, I've carried hundreds of people in my time. I'm not surprised Excelsior chose you to be his flyer. How about one swoop around the mountain for old times' sake?'

Nia leapt up into the air, but as they started to make their way down, Joanna caught sight of Giovanni making his way out of a cave she hadn't noticed before. What was he doing all the way up there? All the dragon caves were on the other side of the mountain. She was going to ask Nia, but

Nia chose that moment to dive down a series of waterfalls and Joanna had to concentrate.

As they flew down the last slope of the mountain, Joanna caught sight of a large van pulling up outside the house. Excelsior was here! And so was Spiky Mike ... Joanna suddenly felt very nervous. Up till now everything had been like a holiday. Had she learned enough to please Spiky Mike? There he was getting out of the van. She took plenty of time to get back to the house, so she could enjoy her final moments of freedom.

As she walked up to the front door it opened and out ran Mouse. 'They're here Joanna. They got here early. Oh, I can't wait to see Excelsior!' Suddenly, neither could Joanna. She glanced over to the van – it was really a lorry and from the ground it looked huge. How much had Excelsior grown in two weeks?

'He's asleep,' called Spiky Mike from the doorway. 'He was so excited I had to sedate him. Still, we're here now. I hope you've been working hard?'

'Extremely,' said Giovanni, coming down the track to join them. 'You've got yourself a good little flyer there.' Joanna felt herself blush and Mouse gave her a little round of applause.

'Glad to hear it,' replied Spiky Mike. 'Well, Giovanni, it's good to see you. You'll be very interested in this dragon.' However, instead of going over to the lorry as Joanna had expected, he turned to go back into the house.

'What about Excelsior? Aren't we going to get him out?' Joanna asked.

'Oh, he'll sleep for a good hour yet,' said Spiky Mike, 'or at least long enough for me to have a drink and something to eat.'

It was early evening by the time Spiky Mike drove the lorry up to the field so that Excelsior could disembark. Everyone had gathered to watch. As the doors opened, Joanna suddenly felt very shy. As she caught her first glimpse of him she gave a little gasp. Excelsior had doubled in size and weight. And his skin was gleaming, shimmering silver in the rays of the evening sun. He looked magnificent, every inch a racing dragon as he walked down the ramp to where Joanna was waiting. To her surprise, he crouched down in front of her. No thoughts, no words, just an invitation to fly. Joanna could feel everyone watching them. She heard Spiky Mike's voice as if from a long way off saying, 'Go on.' She walked round to the side, just as Giovanni had taught her and climbed on to the dragon's back. He was much leaner than Nia and much stronger! As if in a dream she leant forward and placed her cheek against the dragon's face, then slowly and steadily she began to ask the questions that would start the mind-blend.

Suddenly the questions fell away to nothing as her mind touched his. She was no longer Joanna. He was no longer Excelsior. The earth fell swiftly away beneath them and the dragon and the girl moved as one being across the slowly deepening blue of the summer evening sky.

Joanna never spoke to anyone about her first flight on Excelsior; she couldn't find the words. As her audience watched her fly up into the sky, they too felt their own hopes and dreams soar skyward.

Spiky Mike was waiting for her outside the cave where Excelsior would be living.

'That was a deep mind-blend. Don't be disappointed if tomorrow that doesn't happen. Dragons are strange creatures; sometimes they allow you in, other times they keep you hovering around on the surface. Even the good-natured ones will play mind-games. Not that I'm saying Excelsior was playing games,' he added quickly, seeing the look on Joanna's face. 'He missed you when you were away.'

Mouse was waiting for her up in her room. Joanna didn't speak but just gave her friend the most enormous hug.

Chapter 14

Ariadne

The next morning Excelsior was indeed back to his normal perky self, Joanna could hardly get a thought in edgeways. He was feeling very pleased with himself and was boasting over how much he'd grown whilst she'd been away. 'Agnes had to ask her grandson to come and help feed me – I've been on five meals a day – said she'd never seen a dragon eat so much or grow so quickly! And I'm still slim, trim and fast!'

'Tell that dragon to shut up and mind-blend,' snapped Spiky Mike. 'We need to get you used to travelling at speed as quickly as possible. It's up the mountain with the pair of you and no "ifs" or "buts". Now get moving!'

Joanna soon discovered that speed meant fast – very fast. It was like being on a roller-coaster, except there was no track, no carriage and no harness. 'I won't fall off, will I? I mean with us flying so fast,' she asked, during her first hair-raising training session. Her slow dreamy rides on Nia had already become a distant memory.

Spiky Mike scoffed, 'Only if you're really stupid and jump. Now try that exercise again. You've got time for one more attempt before lunch. If you want to stay dry you'll have to be quick. Giovanni says it's going to rain – not that a bit of water should be an obstacle. Racing takes place in all weathers, so you might as well get used to it.' Joanna climbed back up on to Excelsior's back and leaned forward. 'One more time for his Lordship, XL, then lunch,' thought Joanna.

'Good, I'm starving!' came the reply. 'I'll be needing double rations at this rate.' They flew up the mountain at top speed. Spiky Mike's instructions were to descend by spiralling down round the mountain gaining speed as they went. They stopped for a moment at the top. Already the mountain was disappearing in wraiths of cloud and Joanna felt the first spots of rain. Thanks to Ms Lupin's outfit she was at least warm.

'Knowing Spiky Mike, he probably arranged the rain 'specially. Come on, let's get down fast.'

They had just completed the second of the spirals when the rainstorm broke. Thick grey clouds closed in all around them and suddenly they were being pelted on all sides by wet driving rain. Disorientated by the clouds they nearly crashed into the mountainside. Excelsior landed with a skid and a bump. They couldn't possibly continue in such a deluge. Suddenly Joanna remembered the cave she'd seen the day before. It couldn't be too far away and they were on the right side of the mountain. She looked around. The rain was making it difficult to see anything, but yes, there it was directly above them, the dark opening of a cave mouth. 'Quick Excelsior, it's just up there.' Together they scrabbled their way up on to a small path that led directly to the cave. Relieved to be out of the storm they made their way inside. It was a much larger cave than they'd supposed, in that it went quite far back into the mountain. They sat down on the ground to wait. At least they were dry; and with luck the rain would soon stop.

Then without warning something happened that made them both jump with fright. The inside of the cave echoed with a cry – a cry so terrible it froze them in their tracks. 'Wh... what ...

what ... was that?' cried Joanna, clinging as tightly as she could to Excelsior. Excelsior himself shook with fear. 'JoJo, that's a dragon – a dragon in pain! Oohh, it's so terrible I can hardly bear it!' and to Joanna's horror Excelsior started to cry out too in a sort of high pitched wail. His tail began to thrash violently from side to side, so that Joanna had to jump aside to avoid being swept on to the cave wall. He was fast becoming hysterical. Instinctively Joanna threw herself up on to his back and holding on for all she was worth she leant forward to press her cheek against his face and began the questions for mind-blending. Slowly the soft rhythm of the questions calmed Excelsior, until he lay, if not peaceful, at least still.

Only then did Joanna have time to wonder where in the cave the other dragon could be. At least it was quiet now. What could be the matter with it? It must be why Giovanni had been up in the cave yesterday. 'But he didn't mention anything about a dragon at the top of the mountain. Is it some kind of secret? And if so, why?' Suddenly Joanna wondered if the dragon was dangerous. She and Excelsior should get out as soon as possible. She looked over to Excelsior. He was in no state to go anywhere. He'd allowed her to calm him down but had put up a wall to anything more. She walked back to the cave entrance. It was still raining. 'Spiky Mike and Giovanni will come out to look for us when we don't come back,' Joanna reassured herself. She decided to wait in the entrance of the cave so that she could stay reasonably dry and keep some sort of look out. 'If the worst comes to the worst and the other dragon decides to make an appearance we'll be able to slip out of the cave more easily.'

In the end she didn't have to wait very long. She was surprised to see only Giovanni hurrying along the path. She ran out to meet him. 'It's all right, we're here in the cave, the rain came and we couldn't see and then we heard this terrible cry and Excelsior was so frightened.' She suddenly stopped. Giovanni was staring at her half in astonishment, half in alarm.

'Joanna, what are you talking about? What are you doing here?'

'Oh,' said Joanna, 'if you haven't come to find us then what ... have you come to see that other dragon? What's the matter with it? Excelsior is terribly afraid.' Giovanni looked down at Joanna, as if he was wondering what to do next. 'Look, let's get out of the rain.' She followed Giovanni back in to the cave. He had lost his usual cheerful smile and instead looked serious and grave. 'What

I am going to tell you is a secret – not because I want it to be, but to protect the dragon until – or rather *if* – she can be healed. I am only telling you now because you have discovered her existence. Her name is Ariadne. She was hatched in one of Marius King's laboratories as part of an experiment which went badly wrong. Spiky Mike discovered her in a disused laboratory. She was only a few days old and had been left to die. He managed to smuggle her out of the caves without detection. He brought her to me and I have cared for her ever since though sometimes I think it would be better if she had died.'

Joanna listened in horror. 'What did Marius King do to her?'

'His so-called expert neurologist was trying to develop a way of genetically changing the nerves in a dragon's brain so that the dragon would be faster, leaner and more powerful. Unfortunately for Ariadne she is now in constant distress and a great deal of pain.'

'So that's why Spiky Mike hates Marius King so much!' exclaimed Joanna. 'And is Marius King still doing those horrible experiments?'

'We presume so. News is already beginning to filter out that they have an extraordinary new dragon and flyer for the next season.'

Joanna remembered the flyer she had seen at Ms Lupin's. 'I've already seen their new flyer – he looks like a champion.'

'Looking like a champion isn't the same as being a champion,' reflected Giovanni, 'although I suppose it helps to know that people believe in you.'

'It's better than people always telling you how young and inexperienced you are,' said Joanna quietly.

Giovanni looked down at Joanna and smiled. 'I think you should be rather proud to be the youngest flyer on the racing circuit. Let's be practical – what have you got to lose? Although I don't think losing is going to be your problem – Excelsior is amazing. He's going to cause quite a stir – and although Marius King is not going to be happy to have his supremacy challenged, the rest of us will be delighted.'

'What about Ariadne?' asked Joanna. 'What will happen to her? Can you make her better?'

'Well, something has happened today, quite by chance, that might help. Due to the distressing nature of her injuries I have always kept Ariadne away from other dragons as they communicate with each other telepathically. You can see for yourself how distressed Excelsior is. However, now that she has communicated with him, he might be able to tell us something that will help her. Will you ask him for me?'

Joanna turned to where Excelsior was lying. His eyes were closed and he was still trembling. 'It won't hurt Excelsior, will it?'

'Hopefully, it will help him too,' said Giovanni.

Joanna sat down close to Excelsior, but as soon as her face touched his cheek to start the mind-blend she could feel Excelsior begin to block his mind.

'XL, we're going to help her. Please let me in, tell me what you know. You might be the only one who can tell us what we need to do.'

Slowly she felt for a tiny gap in the wall of Excelsior's mind. She sensed more than heard him sob. 'There's too much ... too much! She needs the fire ...'

'Too much? What do you mean? What fire?'

'Ask Vincent ...' She came out of the mind-blend with a jolt as Excelsior snapped down the barrier of his mind.

She turned back to Giovanni. 'He must mean the silver fire that I saw once in Vincent's study. He told me it can change things – I didn't really understand, but I know Excelsior was born in it.'

'Vincent Marlowe?' Giovanni looked thoughtful. 'Very well, I'll give him a ring as soon as we get back. I'll just check Ariadne's food supplies and then we'll go back down.' Joanna nodded and walked over to the cave entrance to wait. It was still raining and the mist hung tightly to the mountainside. Somewhere down below the real world was continuing. She wondered what her parents were doing – probably visiting some castle while her brother would be tearing up and down some football pitch. Just ordinary everyday things; she suddenly missed them so much. Wave after wave of homesickness swept over her. How had she got mixed up in this strange world? She looked back to where Excelsior was still lying with his eyes closed. 'It's all your fault,' she hissed, 'if you hadn't chosen me I could be back home with my friends!' Joanna stopped. What was she saying? 'No! I love flying and when we beat that *horrible* man's dragon I'll laugh and laugh!'

'Joanna, I'm ready,' Giovanni's voice called her back from her thoughts. 'Do you think Excelsior is ready to fly yet? Spiky Mike must be wondering where you are.'

'We can't have that, can we?' snapped Joanna walking back to where Excelsior was still lying by the cave wall. 'Come on XL, time to get back to Mr Bossy Boots! He might let you have some dinner – if you're lucky!'

'Joanna! Are you feeling OK?' asked Giovanni in alarm. 'You don't sound ...'

But Joanna had already gone

Chapter 15

The Alchemist's Fire

'What do you mean, you couldn't see where you were going?' stormed Spiky Mike. He was furious at Joanna's failure to complete the descent down the mountain according to his instructions.

'You should have flown more slowly and not so close to the mountainside. And don't go blaming that dragon; I told you that races happen in all sorts of weather. I'll give you an hour for lunch and then I expect you and Excelsior to do that exercise again until I am satisfied.'

Joanna jumped off Excelsior's back and stomped off towards the house without a backward glance.

Spiky Mike tore after her, stopping her in her tracks. 'Come back immediately! You can't just leave Excelsior and swan off for your own lunch. He needs to be flown back to his cave and fed!'

Joanna exploded, '*Fly* him yourself! You haven't even asked if either of us is OK. We found that dragon up the mountain with its brain all mashed up – and all you can do is shout. Don't you care?'

Spiky Mike turned pale. 'What! You found Ariadne?' but Joanna wasn't listening. She pushed past him into the house and ignoring Mouse, ran straight up to her room. Slamming the door behind her as hard as she could she threw herself on to her bed and let herself cry hot, hard tears.

She must have fallen asleep because when she woke up it was dark. She sat up. Mouse was sitting on the bed opposite watching her.

'I suppose they sent you up to spy on me,' Joanna snapped at her friend, but Mouse just shook her head. 'I made them tell me what it was all about. Do you think Vincent Marlowe will be able to help Ariadne? Spiky Mike phoned him while you were asleep. He should arrive sometime tomorrow … Joanna, he's very upset, you know.'

Joanna shrugged her shoulders angrily. 'I presume *he* is Spiky Mike – well so he should be! I hate him – *Joanna, do this, do that now! Now! Now!*' The tears splashed down her cheeks, but she brushed them angrily aside.

Mouse stuffed a tissue into her friend's hand. 'Lucia said that Spiky Mike was the one who rescued Ariadne.'

'Tell me something I don't already know,' said Joanna haughtily.

'He had to sneak her past Marius King's security guards.'

'I'm sure that wasn't too difficult – he was chief trainer.'

'And then he had to give up his job and break off with his girlfriend. Lucia says …'

'Lucia seems very keen all of a sudden to tell all the gossip,' snapped Joanna. Mouse stared in disbelief at her friend. 'Joanna, what's the matter with you? Why are you like this? Don't you know how lucky you are to have Spiky Mike train you?'

'So everyone keeps telling me. Funny thing is I don't think so. Now why don't you go back down to them? Go and be with those nice grown-ups. You can tell them I'm NOT coming down.'

Joanna threw herself back down on the bed. She heard Mouse say, 'Yeah, whatever,' followed by the slam of the door as Mouse left the room. Joanna was alone and she was glad.

The next morning, she woke up with a terrible headache. Was she ill? She looked down to see that she was still dressed in her flying suit. Suddenly the memory of the previous day came flooding back. Had she said all those terrible things? She looked across to Mouse's bed. It was empty. Joanna knew she must have upset her terribly. 'But why should I apologize, I was right, I know I was!' No! She wasn't, she'd been angry and rude. She'd better go and apologize. Joanna tried to get out of bed, and instantly put her hands to her head. It felt as if someone had sliced it open with a knife. She fell forwards and crashed into the door. Then there were footsteps hurrying along the corridor followed by Lucia's voice asking, 'Joanna, are you all right?'

The door opened. Lucia took one look at Joanna and immediately called for help …

Joanna had the sensation of travelling very fast along a thin tunnel towards a bright light that suddenly overwhelmed and filled every part of her. And then she was part of the light and the light was everywhere and in everything. Suddenly it started to burn hotter and hotter all around her. Things she couldn't name were melting, dissolving and then burning up until all that was left was – her.

She opened her eyes. There was Vincent and he was smiling. 'Hello Joanna, you gave us quite a scare.'

'Vincent! You're here! Then how long is it since …? All I can remember is my head hurting and I couldn't stand up and I said terrible things … it was horrible.'

'It would appear that when the dragon, Ariadne, called to you for help up in the cave you mind-blended with her unintentionally. The chaos of her mind obviously overloaded yours; bringing to the surface all sorts of things you normally keep hidden.'

'But I was so horrible – I didn't even know I felt any of those things.'

'Ah, we all keep secrets, especially from ourselves. Don't feel too bad about it,' and then Vincent added with a smile, 'I hear you gave Spiky Mike quite an earful – it will have done him the world of good to be on the receiving end.'

'What did you do to me?' asked Joanna somewhat nervously.

'Quite simply' said Vincent, 'I made a fire and used it to purify your mind just enough to restore its balance.'

'The silver fire that I saw in your study?'

'Yes,' replied Vincent, 'the same one.' Joanna nodded. She had no conscious memory of the fire, but she could still feel it, just below the surface of her mind.

'Vincent, why was I the only one to be affected by Ariadne? I mean Giovanni visits her everyday.'

'It would appear that you have an extraordinary natural ability when it comes to mind-blending with dragons and when Ariadne called, you experienced her pain.'

'What about Excelsior?' Joanna asked anxiously.

'He heard her too.'

'Spiky Mike has been keeping a close eye on him and he seems fine, but just to be on the safe side I will make my fire for him as well. Now stop worrying and get some rest; I've got some dragons to see.' He was turning to go when Joanna suddenly called after him, 'Vincent!'

'Yes, my dear?'

'Thank you.'

As soon as they would let her, Joanna got up. Apart from anything else she was starving hungry. But first she went to hug Mouse (that was the easy bit) and then she wanted to see Spiky Mike. He wasn't around the house and Joanna hoped he wasn't trying to avoid her.

'Not at all,' said Lucia, as she put a huge bowl of soup down in front of Joanna. 'He's just gone up to the caves to feed the dragons, whilst Giovanni has taken Vincent up to see Ariadne. You can go and find him AFTER you've eaten this.'

Later, Mouse walked up the mountainside to the caves with Joanna and they talked about everything that had happened – and especially Ariadne.

'Did you see her?' asked Mouse, 'apparently she's a Crimson Flame Dragon; they're a very sleek and graceful dragon.'

'No, I didn't see her at all,' Joanna replied. She looked up to the top of the mountain, to where she knew the cave must be. 'I wonder if Vincent's made his fire yet and if it will work?'

Before long the girls reached the caves. Mouse said she would wait outside; so Joanna left her friend to practise her handstands and made her way into the caves. She soon found Spiky Mike. He had just finished feeding Nia and was rinsing out the bucket with water. Joanna stood in the entrance to the cave, not quite sure what to say. He looked over at her and nodded. 'You feeling better now?'

She nodded back, then said, 'I just wanted to say I'm sorry.' To her surprise Spiky Mike looked genuinely astonished. 'It was hardly your fault.' Then it was Joanna's turn to be amazed, because he went on, 'I probably deserved it. I forget how young you are sometimes – and don't think I'm insulting you saying that. You're going to give

Marius King a really good run for his money this next racing season on Excelsior but it's going to be tough and I want you well prepared. Now, how about …'

But Joanna never found out what he wanted her to do as Mouse came running into the cave shouting, 'Oh, come and see, come and see. Vincent's done it!'

They followed Mouse out on to the mountainside and looked to where she was pointing. Coming down the mountain were Giovanni and Vincent but high above them a shimmer of crimson was slowly flying in and out of the clouds – Ariadne!

Chapter 16

Correspondence

'What's this, Frederick?' asked Marius King, picking up the file that Dr Alexander had just placed on his desk.

'It's a fax from Giovanni Balivo to Dr Adam Mundy.'

'And that's important because …?'

'Look at the title'

Marius King opened the file and read, '*Report on Ariadne, Crimson Flame Dragon*'. He quickly flicked through the report. 'So Spiky Mike took the dragon up to Balivo's sanctuary did he? I suppose I should have guessed. But they still can't prove the dragon had anything to do with us.'

'Of course they can't; after I'd bypassed that little

"problem" of brain scrambling I destroyed all the notes,' replied Dr Alexander. 'But Marius, read the end of the report. What do you think of that?'

Marius King turned to the final page and frowned, '*Vincent Marlowe* has "cured" the dragon with a special fire?'

Dr Alexander shook his head. 'I don't know what it means either. But the more normal the dragon, the better for us.'

'Even so, we don't want Adam to see this report,' replied Marius King. 'You are sure he doesn't know about it?'

'Not a chance. He was out of the office getting some ice for our drinks when it arrived. As soon as I saw the title page I knew I had to *remove* it.'

'That was quick thinking on your part, Frederick,' said Marius King. 'But we're going to have to do something about Balivo. He's going to want to see some action taken by the WDRF.'

Dr Alexander grinned. 'Actually I sent back a message immediately saying the WDRF would contact him if they needed any further information.'

'And I think we should get Adam out of the way for a bit just in case Balivo tries to contact him again. Why not invite him to be your guest on your trip to the States?'

'I'll do it straight away,' said Dr Alexander

Marius King closed the file. 'Problem sorted! How fortunate you were to be in the right place at the right time.'

After Dr Alexander had gone Marius King took his nightly stroll around the caves. Normally this was his favourite part of the day. Everyone else had gone home and he could survey his empire in peace. Only tonight his mood was definitely not tranquil. He was irritated. He was going to have to tighten up security. Spiky Mike must have smuggled that dragon out of the caves somehow. 'From now on I must be sure that nothing enters or leaves these caves without my knowing.' He walked along the passageways of the caves considering new security measures until finally he found himself outside Prometheus' cave. He stopped. A voice was coming from inside the dragon cave. Who was there without permission so late at night? He slipped silently into the cave. It was dark, but he could just make out the shape of a person in the green glow that radiated from Prometheus' body. Hardly daring to move, lest he should cause a disturbance, he slowly moved further in to the cave. Hannibal was crouched down next to Prometheus. He was deep in a mind-blend; his lips and face moving in perfect synchronisation with the dragon's.

Marius King was impressed, but he knew Hannibal was there unofficially. He waited until Hannibal had broken the mind-blend then he walked forward to touch Hannibal on the shoulder. Hannibal started at the contact, then realising who it was he let out a visible sigh of relief. 'Marius, I thought you were Afra. She doesn't like me mind-blending too deeply with Prometheus when she's not there. But I have to. He's calling me to go deeper. I know the deeper I go, the faster I'll fly.'

'Really,' said Marius King. 'Tell me more.'

'I used to start with the normal mind-blend questions, but now we just skip those. Now I can go straight to the heart of his mind and I can feel the fire there. Marius, it's pure power.'

Marius King smiled at the young man. He understood power. Silently he put his fingers to his lips. Hannibal's secret was safe with him. 'I'll deal with Afra. You have my permission to be here any time, day or night. But if your little secret is to stay one, I suggest you get a good night's sleep. You look exhausted.'

'Hey man, I'm fine, really! Just a slight headache, nothing that a bit of fresh air won't put right. OK!' Hannibal shrugged his shoulders and hurried out of the cave ahead of Marius King.

Prometheus watched them go. The young man

was right. Inside him there was power. His dragon power. Funny how he could dangle it tantalisingly in front of him like some shiny trinket. Did humans think they could share power with a Jewel Dragon? Oh foolish ones! Jewel Dragons always took all. It was their nature. Everyday now he gained a little more control of the young man's mind. It was fun to have some sport and he had plenty of time. And thanks to that doctor's experiment, he had twice the capacity of any other dragon. It was really quite wonderful.

Blackpool Tower Dragon Caves

Blackpool Tower, Central Promenade,
Blackpool.

5 September

Dear Joanna,

I've been back home 5 whole days and this is the first chance I had to write to you. Because ... I am now the owner (well my parents are really) of a dragon! Can you guess?? Yes! Ariadne!!! I can hardly believe it myself. After you left Wales it was so quiet and I missed you soooo much that to cheer me up Lucia asked me to take Ariadne for a fly. She flies quite slowly so I thought wouldn't she be perfect for my circus acrobatics. And when I asked her she said 'yes, why not!' Joanna, I showed her my routine and she knew exactly what to do! She made some really good suggestions that helped me a lot. I kept everything a secret until the last evening and then I arranged a show with music and everything for my family and Lucia and Giovanni. They were so amazed and everyone clapped and then best of all Giovanni said there was no way he could separate us now and would my Dad be prepared to accommodate one more dragon in the Tower caves. Of course he said 'yes!'

Jo, I know you'll be coming up to Blackpool for

the novice race, but please come sooner. I asked Dad and he said you can come up and train the week before and practise flying over the sea. Oh please ask Vincent and Spiky Mike. Write back soon or phone OR ANYTHING!

Lots of love, Mouse xxxx

P.S. Give my love to Excelsior

jojo
vincnt & spky mke sed yes as lng as its ok with yr dad!!
& i hav 2 train proply

acrobatmouse07
gr8! whos comin

jojo
all of us - vincnt, spky mke
& agnes says she ♥ blakpool

acrobatmouse07
i thought she was trning an egg at the mo

jojo
her grndson isaac will look after
it
how's ariadne
I fort spky mke was gng to cri
when i told him u wr lookin after
hr

acrobatmouse07
Can't w8 til u c hr. she get's
beta evrydy
But 2moro I'm bac at skool
When r you bac

Jojo
i'm not!!!!!
vincnt's going 2 tch me!!!.he's v
clevr
i don't fink he'll be v strict
spky mke is rlly pleased-says i
was wastng 2 much time going 2
skool b4n time 4 more mnd blndng
aaahhhh
lol

Part 3

THE RACES

The Bonfire Night Novice Race - 5 November

Chapter 17

Novice Racers

The Bonfire Night Novice Race was always the first race of the season. An essentially British tradition in the international world of dragon racing, it took place every 5 November in Blackpool just as the town's illuminations were finishing. As its name suggested the race was for flyers and their dragons who had never raced in a WDRF race before.

'Lucky for us that Mouse invited you up early,' said Spiky Mike as they made their way onto a deserted beach up at Rossall where the Blackpool dragons always trained. 'The novice race starts with a take-off from the beach itself and as you can see from the waves today, things can get quite rough.'

It was very windy and the waves were tossing up huge white heads of spray. Poor Excelsior found it very disconcerting and kept mis-timing his starting leap so that they seemed to fly through the waves rather than over them. Before long Joanna was soaking wet.

'I hope you're not flying through the waves on purpose XL,' said Joanna. 'Not at all,' said Excelsior, 'I've got water up my nose and salt stinging my eyes.'

'Watch Mouse and Ariadne – they just wait that extra second before they go,' shouted Spiky Mike over the spray.

'Not on purpose,' hissed Mouse, 'it's just that we're naturally slower than you.'

'I heard that, Mouse,' said Spiky Mike. 'Just learn the lesson Joanna, and remember our first race is next week, not next month.'

Next week soon became next day. All along the promenade people had erected welcoming tents and food tents and drinks tents and each one was full of officials all wearing WDRF badges and wanting to see ID. Joanna knew some of the other flyers and their dragons had already arrived. She got out her programme and for the umpteenth time read through the list of flyers.

She rather liked the look of Oisin and Fearghall,

the McQuinn twins; a pair of stunt men in their early twenties, who had flown over from the West coast of Ireland. They were hoping to add dragon racing to their list of skills. She'd seen them walking along the promenade and they were both identical. She wondered if they flew identical dragons. They seemed to have befriended the glamorous Chloe Benjamin who had flown in from the States for the race. Mouse had also told her to look out for a young Australian called Chris Perry, also known as Crispy, because a dragon had once tried to eat his blond curls. The dragon had left only a few frazzled hairs on his head. The curls had grown back but the name had stuck.

But it was obvious who the centre of attention was. The only flyer most people were really interested in was Hannibal Henry Oliver. There was a double-spread colour photo of him in the November edition of *Dragon Fire* magazine and Blackpool was full of girls awaiting his arrival.

'I don't suppose we'll see the Brighton Caves' team until the very last moment,' said Spiky Mike. 'They've kept all details about their dragon a closely guarded secret and I expect Marius King is going to want to make a grand entrance. Although I'm surprised he's decided to miss the "Fly by Night".'

'What's that?' asked Joanna intrigued. 'Oh let me tell her please!' pleaded Mouse.

'No!' laughed Spiky Mike, 'it's a surprise!'

'Give me just a tiny clue!' cried Joanna.

'No,' said Spiky Mike. 'Just be in Excelsior's Cave at 7.00.'

'It's not more mind-blending, is it?' asked Joanna suspiciously.

'Wait and see!'

But when Joanna arrived at the cave Excelsior wasn't there. 'Don't look so worried Joanna, he's waiting for you ... somewhere, and then you're going for a little fly.' At his words Mouse nearly fell over laughing. 'Just a little fly!' she echoed. 'Go on Jo, and don't forget to wave.' 'Come on,' said Spiky Mike, 'or we'll be late.'

Spiky Mike drove along the Blackpool streets until he came to the airport where he stopped to park. 'Tonight is the last night of the Blackpool illuminations and all the competitors in the Novice Race have been invited to "fly" them. Over on the runway you'll find Excelsior waiting for you. Now hurry up, everyone's waiting.'

As Joanna walked onto the runway she could sense from the beat of leathery wings circling around her that the sky was full of dragons. Soon she and Excelsior were flying up among them. Like a great flock of birds they turned as one to follow the breathtaking river of coloured and sparkling lights snaking its way along the promenade!

And then it was race day.

Joanna spent the early part of the day going over race tactics with Spiky Mike. 'The big unknown in all of this is the Brighton Pavilion Dragon. It's bound to be fast, but then so is Excelsior. Take an early lead and stay there and if it comes to a sprint finish for the line give Excelsior a free rein to go for it.'

Joanna's family had come up for the race and while Vincent and Agnes waited for them to arrive Spiky Mike and Joanna went to complete their registration. 'I'll officially register Excelsior and take him down to the start, while you go and get changed. When you're ready just follow the sign that says flyers' enclosure. I'll be waiting for you there.'

She was glad she wasn't the only one in the female changing area; Chloe Benjamin and another young woman had already changed and were admiring the beading on each other's jackets. They smiled at Joanna and showed her where she could change. Joanna had tried on her flying outfit countless times since it had arrived from Ms Lupin's but now that the moment had come to put it on for real she felt such a tingle of excitement. As she zipped up her jacket she stared at her reflection in the mirror and this time it was her own voice she heard say, 'Dragon Flyer.' She came out of her changing room to find the other two flyers had waited for her. 'We girls ought to stick together,' Chloe Benjamin smiled, 'are you ready?'

Joanna nodded and followed them out. As they entered the enclosure it seemed that pandemonium had broken loose. Joanna felt her heart sink as she recognised the voice shouting the loudest – Spiky Mike. He was in a full-blown argument with Afra Power.

'You know perfectly well that Jewel Dragons are dangerous, vicious creatures! What do you mean Madame Akua herself signed the documentation?' Suddenly Spiky Mike found himself surrounded by WDRF officials. Fortunately, Vincent arrived just at that moment and managed to persuade Spiky Mike to come and meet Joanna's family. Moments later pandemonium broke out a second time with the arrival of Hannibal Henry Oliver and his entourage. A television crew leapt in to action and their very attractive presenter sidled up to Hannibal's side. Joanna recognised her as Sherelle Davis, the front woman for the TV programme

Dragon Racing Today. 'Hannibal, everyone is so excited about your first race and the first public appearance of your dragon. Please tell our viewers about Prometheus.'

Hannibal turned directly to the camera. 'He is power, pure power.' He gave a quick wave, before making his way over to a group of young girls to sign autographs.

'My, what a handsome young man!' Joanna heard her mother say. 'Joanna he looks rather good. What's his name?'

'Mum!' said Joanna indignantly, 'You're supposed to be supporting me!'

'That's Hannibal Henry Oliver, he's from the Brighton Pavilion Caves and they're present champions,' added her father. 'I've read all about them.' Joanna gaped at her brother for support, but even he seemed equally impressed by Hannibal. 'He's favourite to win today you know, and look who's with him, that's the rapper Zane Smythe. He's just been five weeks at the top of the US charts; hey, d'you think I can get his autograph?'

Just then the voice over the tannoy announced that all flyers and trainers should make their way to the start. Joanna was positively relieved to say her goodbyes!

They had drawn the middle lane. 'To make sure

you don't get boxed in you'll need to fly out high and fast, and as for that Jewel Dragon, keep away from it at all costs. It will try to force the other competitors to fly wide so be aware of your own position,' advised Spiky Mike. Joanna climbed up on to Excelsior's back and waited for Spiky Mike to make his final checks. Little sparkles of reflected light from the sun shining on the sea were making Excelsior's scales shimmer. 'They look like my tummy feels,' thought Joanna, 'like a million butterflies flapping around.'

A siren sounded. 'Right, that's my signal to leave,' said Spiky Mike. 'It's five minutes to the start of the race. Remember everything we've practiced. I'll be waiting here for you at the end of the race.'

Joanna was rather surprised that he hadn't said good luck or do your best; until it occurred to her that he was as nervous as she was.

Now it was just her and Excelsior: their first race! To her right and left were the other competitors. All novice flyers! All novice dragons! And up on the promenade everyone watching and waiting …

The second siren sounded. Joanna pressed her face against Excelsior. She could feel his excitement: 'Ooh this is it; our first race! I do hope we win, I don't like the look of that dragon to our right.'

Joanna began to panic. What if he started playing up when she started the mind-blend questions? She knew she couldn't afford to even think like that. Slowly, like so many hundreds of times before, she started to ask the questions that would begin the mind-blend. She was grateful they were like second nature, for they calmed her and the dragon until all at once they thought as one.

Almost immediately the starting siren sounded and with a great leap Excelsior shot up into the air. Instantly Joanna was aware of the other dragons all around her. She noted their position, just as Spiky Mike had told her to. Already the giant wingspan of the Jewel Dragon was forcing some of the other dragons to fly slightly over to one side. He wasn't going to move for anyone. Following her thoughts, Excelsior flew up higher. But Prometheus already knew his advantage and followed them upward until he was flying alongside them. They soon left the other dragons behind. This race was already between the two caves: Brixton versus Brighton. Prometheus kept coming in close causing terrible air turbulence for Excelsior. Reluctantly Joanna and Excelsior had to move over to their left. Prometheus was now in the lead and with nothing to hinder him he put on a great burst of speed. Quickly Excelsior raced after Prometheus, taking care to fly directly behind him, but much lower down. They wouldn't give him the opportunity to force them off their course again. Prometheus couldn't have seen them and thinking he had left everybody far behind he gradually dropped his speed. Excelsior matched him; tactics would be everything in this race. And so they flew along at a steady pace until Joanna could see that the half-way mark was fast approaching. And with it would come the 180° turn. If they could stay hidden during the turn they would have the advantage of surprise in the race for home. Suddenly Joanna knew what to do. 'XL, drop right down until we're just skimming the water. They still think they're all alone but if they do look round, chances are they won't look down at the sea. Once we've made the turn, fly up high very quickly. We'll keep just behind them until the last minute, and then race them straight for the finish.'

It turned out to be quite a tricky manoeuvre, and a couple of times Excelsior had to swerve upwards to miss an extra large wave. However Prometheus and his flyer seemed oblivious to what was going on a hundred feet below them and they made the turn around the half-way mark without even glancing down. Immediately Excelsior began his ascent and soon they were high up in the cover of the clouds.

As soon as he was sure they were completely hidden from view Excelsior put on a great burst of speed and for the first time in the race Joanna felt they were now flying as they'd planned – fast. She felt the thrill of speeding through the white clouds and the bursts of golden sun that shone with a shimmering light on Excelsior's scales. For a few seconds she allowed herself to forget that somewhere below them the Jewel Dragon and his flyer were speeding ahead of them towards the finish. 'Can't you feel at all where Prometheus is?' asked Joanna at last.

'Not at all. He's put a mind-block up,' replied Excelsior. 'But I think we should descend now. I can go much faster if I need to.' Immediately Excelsior went into a steep dive; there was no stopping for anyone now. As they broke from the cloud they found they had travelled further than they'd realised. Blackpool Tower – which marked the finish of the race – was just a little way ahead but even so the Jewel Dragon was nowhere in sight. Joanna felt a pang of disappointment. She'd so wanted to win. She could only hope that Vincent and Spiky Mike wouldn't be too disappointed. Excelsior was now flying so low that Joanna could make out the faces of people in the crowd. Everyone was pointing up at them and shouting. They flew round the tower; last night it had been covered in its fairy lights, now it loomed over her sombre and dark against the sky. At least they hadn't come last.

They flew back down to the start. There was nobody there. Where was Spiky Mike? Joanna climbed down off Excelsior's back. 'We were supposed to come back here, weren't we?' asked Joanna. At that moment they heard the sound of running. It was Spiky Mike. To Joanna's utter amazement he picked her and swung her around. 'You won! You won!'

'We won? But what about Prometheus?'

'Prometheus was only just crossing the line as I was making my way down here. Marius King is fuming, calling for an inquiry. Don't worry about him, right now you two are wanted in the winner's enclosure.'

It was all Joanna could do to make a decent enough mind-blend to fly Excelsior the short distance to the winner's enclosure she was shaking so much. They'd won! They'd actually won! Look, there was the Brixton Dragon Caves' flag flying from the winner's flagpole. Joanna could see Vincent and Agnes standing next to Madame Akua and other representatives from the WDRF. As Joanna slipped off Excelsior's back cameras flashed all around her. Madame Akua stepped forward to shake Joanna's hand and to place a medal around her neck and there was a huge winner's rosette for Excelsior.

Then suddenly there was Sherelle Davis standing alongside her. 'Today everyone was expecting a great win from Marius King's new team, but it would appear there is a challenger to the crown. For the past few years the Brixton Caves have been in the doldrums, but now Vincent Marlowe has bred a very fast racing dragon whose potential was enough to persuade champion trainer Spiky Mike Hill to join the Brixton Caves. Of course the great unknown in the equation is their new flyer. Easily the youngest person on the circuit, she was just an unknown schoolgirl until she was discovered by the dragon Excelsior and here she is, Joanna Morris.' Sherelle pushed a microphone under Joanna's nose. 'Well, Joanna that was quite a surprise win you had there. Would you like to tell our viewers how it feels?'

'It's fantastic,' said Joanna, blushing madly as cameras flashed and clicked around her. She stood there desperately trying to think of something to say, 'I fly a wonderful dragon. I mean Excelsior is …'

'Yes, people are talking about records being

broken!' beamed Sherelle Davis, flashing a smile at the camera. But instead of letting Joanna say anything else, Sherelle straightaway went on to say, 'It looks like there is a great season of racing ahead of us. Hannibal H_2O Oliver will not be happy with today's result but I for one can't wait until the next time we see these two extraordinary dragons, Prometheus and Excelsior, battling it out for first place. This is Sherelle Davis reporting for *Dragon Racing Today*.'

Joanna was thankful to escape and made her way over to Vincent. He was beaming from ear to ear. 'Congratulations, my dear! What can I say? What a day for the Brixton Caves! I am so very proud of you! And Excelsior was quite astonishing, even faster than I'd dared imagine. Thank you. Now, allow me the honour of introducing Madame Akua, the President of the WDRF.' Madame Akua turned to Joanna with a smile. 'Congratulations again "JoJo", if I may call you by your flyer's name. Quite a dramatic race for a beginner, especially disappearing into the clouds like that!'

Joanna looked up at her surprised. 'You could see all that?'

'There's a satellite that relays the race to a series of big screens – people didn't know what to think. It was obvious to everyone that Prometheus hadn't spotted you and he thought he could fly at a pace to suit himself. Well, he'll know for next time! Congratulations again to the Brixton Caves. Vincent, I couldn't be more pleased for you. Now go and enjoy your success!' Madame Akua stopped to congratulate Spiky Mike and Agnes before making her way into the enclosure for second place where Marius King was standing with Afra Power and Hannibal. They all stood in a sullen silence. On seeing Madame Akua approach, Hannibal slouched moodily away and went and sat on Prometheus' back; Afra stood staring angrily after him. Marius King however greeted Madame Akua with a smile and a shrug of the shoulders. They turned to look first at Prometheus, then over to where Excelsior was still having his photograph taken, and enjoying it thoroughly. Marius King obviously said something about him to Madame Akua who nodded. Then Joanna felt Marius King's gaze turn upon her as if he were taking in every detail about her. It was a look of pure hatred.

'And I don't like you, either,' thought Joanna. A cold shiver run through her as she quickly turned away and went back to see Excelsior. 'Oh, JoJo, I've just had my photograph taken for the next month's *Dragon Fire* magazine. The photographer said I was the finest Silver Spiked-Back she'd ever seen. Isn't winning great!'

'Yes XL, but I think we'd better enjoy it while we can. I think next time will be very different. Did you see that horrid Marius King looking at you? He knows how fast we can fly now and next time Prometheus and his flyer aren't going to let us out of their sight. Next time I think it will be what everyone is talking about: a race for the line!'

Chapter 18

Defeat

New Year's Day Derby - 1 January

Apart from the Bonfire Night Novice Race the main British racing season was made up of four major races: the New Year's Day Derby, the Valentine Chase, the Easter Extravaganza and the May Day Marathon. Dragons qualified for these races by competing in a series of minor races. The winners of the major races were invited to take part in the Independence Day Speed Trials, an international event that was always held in San Francisco. Here champions from all over the world were invited to race for the title of WDRF Supreme Champion.

As winner of the Bonfire Night Novice race

Joanna had automatically qualified for the New Year's Day Derby but it was still back to the grindstone, at least as far as Spiky Mike was concerned. With Vincent's help he arranged a careful programme of races that would challenge Joanna and Excelsior, but would not exhaust them

Although it turned out quite by chance that Excelsior was entered into different races from Prometheus, rumours abounded that one or other of the caves was avoiding a second confrontation in a minor race. Denials quickly followed on both sides. But nothing would squash the speculation. Joanna was astounded to read in one racing magazine that she had 'developed a crush on Hannibal and couldn't bear to fly against him!'

Both caves dominated their races, easily outstripping their rivals. People started to watch the times and compare them. Excelsior thought it exciting, but Prometheus inwardly seethed. How he hated that girl flyer and her skinny, slither of a dragon. Oh yes, he'd felt its thoughts after the Novice race: stupid carefree thoughts. Well, he would exact his revenge on all of them. He punished Hannibal too for the humiliation of losing and had refused to deep mind-blend until the young man had wept and pleaded for forgiveness. Hannibal vowed to the dragon that nothing would stop him from annihilating his rival next time they met. He began to blatantly ignore Afra's training schedule, preferring to deep mind-blend with the dragon for hours at a time. Afra went to Marius King only to find that he defended his flyer's actions.

'Afra, I must confess that I was disappointed with the result of the Novice race, a result for which you, as Hannibal's trainer, must bear responsibility. Hannibal has already told me that you are preventing him performing a deep mind-blend with the dragon if you aren't there …'

'I'm not saying Hannibal shouldn't,' interrupted Afra, 'I just think he should be carefully supervised – Jewel Dragons are renowned for their fierceness.

Marius King's eyes flashed ice cold across his desk at Afra. 'If I remember rightly you had reservations about my decision to race a Jewel Dragon. Perhaps you recall my saying this venture was not for the faint-hearted. I hope you're not getting cold feet because there are plenty of trainers out there who would jump at this opportunity …'

'No Marius, of course not …'

'Good! Well I suggest that you train Hannibal so that he can mind-blend as much as he likes – and remember, I want results!'

By the time the New Year's Day Derby arrived the dragon racing world was at fever pitch. Vincent had to hire security men to guard the Brixton Caves from would-be fans eager for a glimpse of Excelsior.

Spiky Mike and Vincent had done everything they could to prepare Joanna and Excelsior for what would be the most difficult flight so far, but nothing could have prepared them for the reception they received on arriving for the race. Although there were ten other caves represented, the spectators seemed to be divided into those supporting Prometheus and those supporting Excelsior and booed or cheered accordingly as Joanna and Hannibal arrived in the flyers' enclosure. The two flyers ignored each other despite numerous calls for a photo. Joanna for her part was desperately trying to stay in control of her nerves. She was aware of Excelsior's constant chattering – something that hadn't happened for a long time – and she knew he too was extremely nervous.

Joanna was relieved to find that Prometheus had drawn an outside lane, whereas they had a central lane. At least they had the starting advantage. The plan was to fly as fast as they could right from the start, rather than try and fly a tactical race. 'Although I imagine that Hannibal and Prometheus will be following a similar plan,' said Spiky Mike. He watched Joanna settle herself down on to Excelsior's back and began to walk away when suddenly he turned and said, 'I don't normally say this, but good luck.'

Joanna knew she would need every bit of luck available to her. She could feel Excelsior trembling beneath her as she leant forward and placed her face close to his. 'XL, I'm going to start the mind-blend. Ready?' To Joanna's horror he didn't reply. Desperately trying to control her rising panic she started to intone, 'First question: What are you?'

To her relief he replied, but she felt as though the answer was coming from a long way off. By the time the starting siren sounded she had managed to ask all four questions, but her hold on his mind was very fragile. She was in a dilemma. To fly out now and risk the mind-blend breaking which would be disastrous or try to get a better mind-blend and start behind everyone else. Were they fast enough to catch up? In reality she knew she had no choice but to strengthen the mind-blend. She continued repeating the four questions again and again, until finally she felt she was able to give the instruction, 'Fly!'

They never stood a chance. Prometheus had taken full advantage of the situation and powered into an early lead. Joanna did everything she could, but they still came in last. She could hear the boos of the disappointed spectators as she came in to land.

Spiky Mike was already waiting for them. He just stood there looking at Excelsior; he was white with anger. 'I'm sorry, I'm sorry,' cried Joanna, as soon as they'd landed 'I just couldn't get him to mind-blend properly. I ...'

'It wasn't you Joanna; that dragon's been tampered with. Anyone can see it. I'm amazed you even got off the ground. Look Joanna, I don't want to leave him unattended, so go up to Vincent and get him to call for security.'

'Tampered with, how?' asked Joanna, aghast.

'I don't know yet! Just do as I say and get Vincent,' snapped Spiky Mike.

'I suppose Prometheus won,' said Joanna.

'Of course; who else!'

Despite a full stewards' inquiry nothing was found to be wrong with Excelsior. All the security tapes were checked and showed that only Spiky Mike and Joanna had had access to Excelsior.

'Nothing, absolutely nothing!' said Vincent, as he read out the findings a week later. All the tests have come back negative. 'I'm sorry but the official verdict is that either Joanna or Excelsior were overcome by nerves.'

'Huh,' snorted Spiky Mike, 'I don't believe that any more than you. No, something happened to Excelsior and I intend to find out! Tell Joanna I need to speak to her when she comes in.'

Joanna arrived to find Spiky Mike talking things over with Agnes. 'There's something staring us in the face about this business and we're walking right past it,' said Agnes.

'Walking past it,' scoffed Spiky Mike, 'I wish I could – it feels more like a brick wall.' 'But that's what it did feel like,' said Joanna, astonished she hadn't thought of it before, 'as though there was a wall between Excelsior and me – not like when Excelsior won't let me mind-blend but as though something else was there, stopping me from communicating with him.'

Agnes looked at the pair of them thoughtfully. 'Is there any way a dragon could control another dragon's thoughts?'

'I've never heard of it,' said Spiky Mike, 'what do you mean?'

'Well, dragons can communicate with each other telepathically if they want to, so if Marius King is experimenting on dragons' brains perhaps he's made it possible for a dragon to affect the mind of another. Like some sort of mind-blend.'

'But it would have to be an extremely strong

mind-blend and I don't think it could hold it for very long,' said Spiky Mike

'Long enough to start a race?' asked Agnes.

'And remember Ariadne was able to affect me and Excelsior and she'd been experimented on,' said Joanna.

Spiky Mike was now almost certain they had found the answer to what had happened. He wasn't worried for Excelsior; once the dragon was aware of such a possibility he would guard against it. No, the real worry was for Hannibal Henry Oliver. If Prometheus was able to prevent another dragon from mind-blending with a flyer even for a short time, what was its influence over its own flyer?

Chapter 19

Tails!

The Valentine Chase – 14 February

Afra was late home after what had been another difficult day. There was a constant tension now between Marius and herself. Her training and her instinct kept on telling her that in flying a Jewel Dragon they were heading for trouble, yet all the evidence pointed to Hannibal having excellent control. Prometheus certainly did not show any signs of violent behaviour so perhaps Dr Alexander really had transformed its aggression into speed. If only she understood more about what had been done to the dragon's brain.

She'd thought of phoning Madame Akua, but

as Madame Akua had signed the registration papers she must believe the dragon was harmless. There was one person who would understand her concerns, but asking *him* was out of the question. It had bothered her more than she cared to admit that Spiky Mike thought the dragon dangerous for she knew his instincts about dragons were usually right. Typically he'd found a magnificent dragon to train, although she had to admit she was surprised by his choice of flyer. She was so young and already it looked as if the pressure was beginning to get on top of her. On the other hand the Silver Spiked-Back Dragon was certainly the only dragon that could possibly challenge Prometheus for speed. Thank goodness Hannibal and Prometheus had won the New Year's Day Derby. If they hadn't, she knew she would have been sacked.

She ran herself a hot bath. Perhaps that would calm her down. She must have half-drifted off in the warmth of the water because suddenly she awoke with a start. The phone was ringing. Before she could get out of the bath to reach it, the answerphone clicked on and with a sudden shock she heard a voice she knew only too well.

'Afra, it's Mike, if you're there pick up.'

Afra's heart gave a little skip; but she hesitated to pick up the phone and he continued with his message. 'We need to talk … about Prometheus and … just phone me.' The phone beeped – he'd hung up. Immediately she pressed the replay button. It was the first time he'd called her since they split up and she didn't know whether to be pleased or angry. She played the message back yet again and knew she was angry. Prometheus was none of his business – especially since the Brighton Caves had won the last race and his dragon had come in last. Marius was right; she'd been making a silly fuss about nothing. Maybe this phone call was just the spur she'd needed. And when Hannibal and Prometheus were made supreme champions *Spiky* Mike would have to admit that she had been right all along!

It was a sign of how worried Spiky Mike was about Prometheus that he'd phoned Afra. Despite their differences she was the only one in the Brighton Caves who might possibly listen to him. And the truth was he still missed her terribly … Still he couldn't afford to think like that, not when he needed to turn his attention to preparing Joanna and Excelsior for the next major race, the Valentine Chase.

For the Valentine Chase, dragons were paired up in a draw. On a siren the first dragon would start flying, exactly one minute later the second dragon would begin to chase after it. If the second dragon caught the first before the final siren – it had to place a red marker on its side – it was the winner, otherwise the first dragon won. It was always a very popular race and this year there were a record number of entries.

Joanna and Excelsior quickly progressed through the early stages to qualify for the main race. They took care not to draw too much attention to themselves and only flew as fast as was necessary. They had one scare, when Lady Danielle Campbell-Lee on her dragon Charlie Boy, dive-bombed them out of the clouds only to find that the final siren had already sounded. Spiky Mike was not pleased, but the incident was enough to jolt the pair out of the false sense of security that lack of real competition had given them.

Prometheus and Hannibal were determined to fly the fastest times and as a result drew the top seeded position. The Brixton Caves were second – 'Which means if WDRF seeding goes to plan, Joanna and Excelsior will fly against Brighton Caves in the final,' said Vincent as he and Spiky Mike went through the official race timetable.

'Yes, inevitable I suppose,' said Spiky Mike. 'I've been keeping a close eye on them in the heats and I have to admit Hannibal is a great flyer and he's handling that Jewel Dragon remarkably well, but I still don't trust Prometheus – especially after what he did to Excelsior last time.'

'Has it occurred to you that whatever procedure they carried out on Prometheus might actually have helped contain his ferocity?' said Agnes, who'd just brought in the morning coffee.

Spiky Mike shook his head. 'I know it looks as if that dragon is under control – but I'm not convinced.'

'I've often wondered if what they've done is that different from Vincent putting Excelsior's egg in an alchemical fire,' argued Agnes as she handed round a plate of chocolate biscuits.

'At least no dragon has suffered at Vincent's hands,' said Spiky Mike, 'and fire is a dragon's natural element.'

Vincent, who had been listening intently, suddenly put down his cup of coffee. 'People misunderstand the fire. It doesn't burn like ordinary fire – rather it has a power to purify excess and as a result transform it. But remember, *"If it is in our power to act nobly, it is also in our power to do evil,"* or so said the Greek philosopher Aristotle. I hope my choice has been for good, otherwise you are right Agnes, I am no better than Marius King and Dr Alexander.'

The Valentine Chase, as its name suggested, took place on 14 February. It was very popular and always well attended. Joanna couldn't quite believe her eyes (or her nose for that matter) when she arrived at the racecourse. Everywhere were huge heart-shaped banks of flowers and all the stands were draped in heart-shaped bunting, but worst of all middle-aged couples were sitting holding hands and looking dewy-eyed at each other. 'Thank heavens Mum and Dad couldn't get time off work!' she thought. To her immense relief she caught sight of Mouse sitting on the steps of one of the stands engrossed in a magazine.

'Hi Mouse,' called Joanna. 'Isn't this most extraordinary thing you've ever seen. I'm glad you're here though. Are you on half-term? My brother doesn't break up till next week.'

'All the Blackpool schools are off this week,' replied Mouse quickly stuffing the magazine in to her bag. But Joanna had already caught sight of what Mouse had been looking at, and she snatched it up to see a full double-page colour poster – a Valentine Special of H_2O himself.

'Mouse! You fancy him, don't you?' Mouse blushed and grabbed it back. 'He's very good looking,' replied her friend sheepishly.

Joanna laughed, but Mouse ignored her and

opening up the magazine again said, 'Actually there's a really interesting article about Spiky Mike and Afra and how they used to go out with each other, but now work for rival caves.' Joanna looked at the article. There were Spiky Mike and Afra, their pictures each side of a huge heart, split in two.

'I've seen them looking at each other, when they think the other one can't see them,' said Mouse. 'I think they still like each other. Watch them today and you'll see what I mean.'

Joanna gazed at her friend quizzically. 'Why are you so interested?'

'Well, Spiky Mike saved Ariadne, and anything to do with her interests me,' said Mouse. 'I've got some more news too. I saw Lucia last week and she told me that the report Giovanni sent to the WDRF had mysteriously disappeared.'

Before Joanna could ask anything else Vincent arrived to tell her it was time to get changed. 'Spiky Mike is waiting with Excelsior. He wants to stay with him at all times you're not racing, just as a precaution.'

Mouse wished her friend good luck, saying, 'You might meet my sister Emilia in the semi-finals, make sure you beat her. She borrowed my new music player last week and she hasn't given it back yet!'

Joanna arrived to find Excelsior in seventh heaven. He'd just received a garland of red paper hearts and flowers bearing his name. 'It's from an adoring fan,' he sighed, 'JoJo I have so many admirers …!'

'I don't think Spiky Mike looks too impressed though. I think he'd prefer it if we got ready to win a few races,' said Joanna.

The races had a carnival feel to them, which was a welcome change to the greyness of the February day. As expected, both the Brighton and Brixton Caves progressed inevitably through their races until the voice over the tannoy announced the race everyone had been waiting for: 'The Grand Final of the Valentine Chase will take place in exactly 30 minutes between the Brighton Pavilion Caves, represented by Hannibal H_2O Henry Oliver, flying the top seed, Prometheus,' (here there was general cheering) 'and the Brixton Caves, represented by Joanna *JoJo* Morris flying the number two seed, Excelsior' (more cheering). At this point a series of small red heart-shaped balloons floated up into the sky and Madame Akua stepped forward to announce that the toss to decide the race positions was now to take place. She called Joanna and Hannibal to either side of her and tossed the coin. Hannibal of course did the gentlemanly thing and insisted that Joanna should call. 'Tails!' said Joanna. It was heads. 'Hannibal, will you fly first or second?' asked Madame Akua. Everyone held their breath; first flyer always had the advantage and Hannibal certainly wasn't going to waste it. 'I'll fly first, Madame Akua.' But the Brixton Caves let out a huge inward sigh of relief. This was what they'd hoped for; Prometheus was such an aggressive chaser that some flyers had literally flown their dragons off the course to avoid him. 'Excelsior has a speed and agility which he hasn't had an opportunity to demonstrate yet, so if you get the opportunity choose to be chaser,' Spiky Mike had told Joanna beforehand.

Before he left Joanna, Spiky Mike checked that Joanna could mind-blend without any interference from Prometheus. 'Clear as a bell?' Joanna nodded. 'Then go get 'em.'

Joanna went straight into the mind-blend with Excelsior. Never before had they wanted to win a race so badly; the pride of the Brixton Caves was at stake. On the first siren Prometheus flew up high in to the sky like a bullet. But Excelsior and Joanna's reactions were equally fast and focussed and on the second siren they too shot up in the sky. Like a streak of silver lightning they raced across the sky in pursuit of their prey. And to everyone's amazement, but not to everyone's delight, they quickly began to gain on them. They were going to catch them! Surely it was not going to be over before it had begun? No, at the last moment Prometheus went into the most dramatic dive, just avoiding Excelsior. Excelsior followed, but instead of diving straight down he started to spiral round and round, but at such a speed that Prometheus was almost caught in the vortex and hardly knew which way to fly. Somehow Hannibal managed to control the dragon so that he soared heavenwards at the very last second. Excelsior gave a flick of his tail and was soon following in pursuit. A murmur rippled through the crowd. Excelsior was faster than Prometheus. The crowd leapt to their feet screaming encouragement; they'd never seen anything like it. And then suddenly the dragons were swallowed up by grey cloud. The crowd groaned. What was happening? No! Look, there they were again. Excelsior had chased Prometheus out of the cloud. How long now till the final siren? It must be only a matter of seconds, and Excelsior was getting closer and closer. They were flying so low that spectators could see the small heart-shaped rosette, which Joanna had to tag onto Prometheus. Suddenly she reached forward – and in that instant it was all over. The small red tag was firmly stuck on Prometheus' backside. The crowd roared and cheered. The Brixton Caves had won the Valentine Chase.

*   *   *   *

Hannibal said afterwards that it was an accident. In all the excitement he hadn't realised that Excelsior was quite so close behind them. Had the tip of Prometheus' tail really hit Joanna as they were coming into land?

He was very concerned and hoped she would make a quick recovery. He'd been told it wasn't too serious, mostly bruising, but unfortunately there would be a small scar under her eye. He was only grateful her helmet had prevented a more serious injury. Yes, he was very much looking forward to racing against her at Easter, if not before.

Part 4

1ST BIRTHDAY

Chapter 20

A Birthday to Remember

Joanna was made to spend the night in a nearby hospital. 'Just as a precaution,' said Madame Akua. 'What an unfortunate accident after such a spectacular victory!'

Joanna was too weak to protest. She had a terrible headache and a bruise covering half her face. The doctor gave her something to help with the pain but it didn't seem to help. She tried to sleep only to find herself disturbed by the sound of voices. She struggled to open her eyes; there was a man in the room. Was it a doctor? He was tall and heavily built but he was standing with the light behind him and she couldn't see his face properly. She knew that she recognised him

– only her head was hurting so much that she just couldn't remember his name … she wished he would go away … he frightened her. She tried to call out for help, but she couldn't. Perhaps she fell asleep because when she opened her eyes again the room was empty.

Next morning she awoke to find her mother sitting next to her bed. 'Darling girl, you're awake at last. How are you feeling? Oh, your poor face. It looks so sore.'

'Mum! You're here!' Joanna tried to smile, but found she couldn't. She sat up to hug her mother. 'Oh, that hurts,' she cried.

'It's going to for a while yet,' said her mum. 'I'm afraid your face is very badly bruised. And you're going to be quite stiff for a few days. Do you want to lie down again?'

'No, I'm OK, now I'm sitting up,' said Joanna. 'Oh Mum, I'm so glad you're here'.

'I got here as soon as I could. It was the middle of the night. Daddy and Aaron both wanted to come but the doctors said it looks worse than it actually is. In fact, if you feel up to it you can come home today after they've given you a final check-over. You've had so many cards and flowers. People are very concerned, you know. Mouse was very upset. And that nice young man, Hannibal, came up to me himself to apologize. It's a shame he couldn't teach that trainer of yours some manners.'

'Spiky Mike,' Joanna replied, wincing as she spoke, she couldn't believe her face could be so sore.

'Honestly, I've never seen a man so angry, why, the air was blue. Kept insisting it was no accident. In the end the hospital authorities had to ask him to leave.'

Her mum's words suddenly reminded Joanna of her night visitor. 'Mum, was there anyone here when you arrived last night?'

'What? In your room? No, they insisted on no visitors so that you could rest, I was only allowed in because I'm your mother. Why?'

'Nothing, I just thought I heard someone.'

'Yes, well, probably that Spiky Mike; you could hear him all along the corridor. The doctor will be coming round shortly, so just lie back and rest till then. I'm just going to go and freshen up.'

As soon as her mother had gone Joanna thought over everything that had happened. Like Spiky Mike she knew that Prometheus had deliberately tried to hurt her. It was only Excelsior's quick thinking that had saved her from being thrown off altogether. She desperately wanted to ask Excelsior what had happened; but of course that would have to wait until she got back to the caves. At least that horrible dragon hadn't hurt him – this time. But what about next time? – she gave a shudder. And that man in her room – she didn't know how Marius King had got there, but she knew it had been him.

Joanna left hospital later that morning. She was shocked to find that a whole host of paparazzi were lying in wait and she had to be smuggled out of a back entrance. 'Fortunately Spiky Mike has already returned to the caves with Excelsior,' sighed Vincent, 'or we *really* might have found ourselves splashed across the front pages of the papers. Still I will have to go and face them and give them a statement saying that you are well, but need peace and quiet to recover fully.'

'Absolutely – peace and quiet!' agreed Joanna's mother.

To Joanna's dismay, she soon discovered that what her mother meant by peace and quiet was forbidding her to go any where near the Brixton Caves! After the first week Joanna was beside herself with boredom and frustration – and she desperately wanted to ask Excelsior about Prometheus' attack.

'Why can't I go? I'm fine and I haven't seen Excelsior for seven whole days!' said Joanna. But her mother had already made her mind up. 'Excelsior can wait a few more days! But if you are beginning to feel a little better you could try catching up on your maths homework. And remember, things are difficult for me as well. I will have a pile of things to catch up on at work and right now I really must go and do a proper shop.'

Joanna knew there was no point arguing with her mother, so she pretended to do her maths until her mother left to go to the supermarket. As soon as she was sure she had really gone Joanna grabbed her jacket and keys and ran out of the house. With luck she could get to the caves, talk to Excelsior and be back before her mum returned – and what she didn't know wouldn't hurt her.

Joanna let herself in through the side door and crept down to Excelsior's cave. She was about to go in when suddenly she heard Spiky Mike's voice through the door. 'I need to get this dragon out flying – surely it's about time Joanna came in – can't you give her a ring?'

Joanna tried not to laugh. It was perfect, she would throw open the doors and shout, 'Here I am!' but Vincent's reply stopped her in her tracks. 'Spiky Mike – I'm sorry, you're not going to like this … For the moment I've asked her mother to keep her at home … No, listen – we have to face the fact that it's all becoming too dangerous for Joanna. We'll have to withdraw her … I'm sorry, but we can't put the child at risk.'

'Withdraw *me*?' Too horrified to move Joanna pressed even closer to the door, ignoring the tears that were falling uncontrollably down her cheeks.

Spiky Mike was not happy either. 'But that's exactly what Marius King wants! And it's Prometheus that should be withdrawn – banned if I had my way! And if not for our sakes, then at least for Hannibal Henry Oliver's!'

'What do you mean?' asked Vincent puzzled.

'After the Valentine Chase, did you not notice that despite all his apologies and show of concern, that underneath it all he looked, well … terrified!'

'Terrified – of what?'

'Of Prometheus! Hannibal knew very well that the dragon deliberately hurt Joanna. Makes you wonder what is really going on in that mind-blend. Jewel Dragons are trouble – always have been, always will be. And I'm telling you, no amount of messing about with that dragon's brain is going to alter its nature – whatever it says in Dr Alexander's fancy notes.'

Joanna was so wrapped up listening to the discussion

behind the cave door that she nearly jumped a mile when a small voice whispered in her ear,

'I have never found it a good idea to listen to conversations that were not intended for me.'

'Oh, Agnes ...' but that was as far as Joanna got before her words were completely swallowed up in all-engulfing sobs. 'My dear child ....' sighed Agnes. 'Let's go back to my office for a cup of tea and then you can tell me all about it'.

Tea with Agnes always took time to prepare. As usual, she carefully set the tray with a lace cloth, a china cup and saucer and a glass and a plate of biscuits. There was no hurrying her as she waited for the tea to brew. Only when she had poured a cup of strong tea and some squash did she sit down and say, 'So Joanna what exactly did you hear?' Somehow through her tears Joanna managed to relay the gist of all she had heard. Agnes was a good listener, and didn't interrupt or comment once. Even when Joanna had finished she took a good few minutes to reply. What she had to say came as a complete surprise.

'What we all need, is to take our time and not rush any decisions that we might regret later. I think we are all in need of a little treat and as it will be Excelsior's birthday in a few days time, why don't you plan a surprise party for him?'

Joanna looked at Agnes in astonishment and amazement. 'What?'

'A birthday party!' smiled Agnes 'With a cake! And perhaps you can put some balloons up in his cave.'

'Oh, he'd love that!' said Joanna half laughing and half crying as she dried her face on the hanky that Agnes had produced, 'he really took a fancy to those red heart-shaped ones we saw at the Valentine Chase.'

As Agnes had suggested, the party was just what every one in the caves needed – a breathing space. Vincent gave it his immediate blessing. He was exceedingly grateful that Joanna had something to occupy her – he only wished his own thoughts could be so easily diverted. It looked as if he would have no option but to withdraw from the racing season. However, he decided to make no final decision until after Excelsior's party.

In the meantime Joanna set about preparing for the birthday party. There were to be two cakes, one for Excelsior made out of creamed chicken livers (his favourite) and a strawberry gateau for everyone else. She wrote out invitations for everyone using Agnes's best pen. And then Agnes and Joanna paid a visit to one of the party shops in Brixton Market to arrange for fifty silver helium balloons to be delivered on the morning of his birthday. They also arranged a presentation of the WDRF ceremonial sash that Excelsior had won at the Valentine Chase. As his contribution to the celebration Spiky Mike went as far as volunteering to collect it from Ms Lupin's on the morning of Excelsior's birthday. As for her own present to Excelsior, Joanna wasn't sure what it should be – except that it should be something she had made herself.

'Can you knit?' Agnes asked her. 'Because a scarf in the Cave colours would look quite fun around his neck.'

'Well I can knit a bit, I learned at school and I know he likes that garland he got at the Valentine race. He puts it on sometimes when he thinks no one is looking. Can you help me with casting-on?'

With a great deal of help from Agnes, Joanna just managed to complete the scarf in time for Excelsior's birthday. It was already half-past nine on the day itself when she hurriedly wrapped it in silver paper (to match Excelsior's scales) and ran out of the house shouting, 'See you all at the party later on.'

She knew that Agnes would be out collecting the birthday cakes, so she let herself in and made her way down to the caves. Vincent's light was on, but the door was closed – a sign that he didn't want to be disturbed, so she left her present in Agnes's office then made her way down to Excelsior's cave. Before Joanna could reach it, however, she heard someone ringing the back door bell. Perhaps the balloons had arrived early. 'The deliveryman must be in a terrible hurry,' thought Joanna as she ran up the stairs because he kept on and on ringing the bell. 'OK! OK' Joanna shouted as she undid the lock, 'Keep your hair on. I'm coming as fast as I can.'

It wasn't the balloons. It was Afra Power! She pushed past Joanna and ran down the stairs. 'Where's Spiky Mike? I've got to find him immediately! Something terrible has happened. I've tried his mobile, but he's not answering.'

Joanna ran down after her. 'He's not here yet. But Vincent's downstairs; perhaps he can help you.'

At the mention of Vincent's name Afra started to yell, 'No, he's not! He's not! Marius has him prisoner. Ever since we returned from the Valentine Chase Hannibal has been acting very strangely, shouting at everyone as well as suffering the most terrible headaches, and then last night he collapsed in Prometheus' cave ...' she shuddered.

'I tried to call for a doctor but Marius said that the person we needed was Vincent Marlowe, because he'd already cured Ariadne. Somebody came and got him …'

Joanna stood there horrified. 'What? Kidnapped him?' How did Marius King know about Ariadne unless … Of course he'd got hold of Giovanni's report! Suddenly it all made sense .

'But now Prometheus won't let any one near Hannibal, especially Mr Marlowe. Spiky Mike is the only trainer I know who might be able to help.'

Thankfully Agnes appeared at that very moment. On hearing Afra's story she hurried down to Vincent's room. It had been turned upside down. All the books and papers from his desk were strewn across the floor. 'This is terrible! Terrible!' muttered Agnes, shaking her head. 'It's the police we should be calling.'

Suddenly Joanna caught a glimpse of her party invitation lying torn on the floor.

Dear Vincent,
You are cordially invited to Excelsior's first Birthday Part...

Excelsior! Perhaps some one had harmed him! She ran out of the office calling, 'Agnes, I need to see Excelsior's all right.'

Joanna ran into the cave. He was there! He hadn't been hurt. She threw her arms around the dragon. 'Oh Excelsior, it's all gone wrong, it's your birthday and we were going to have a birthday party with balloons and a cake, but Marius King has kidnapped Vincent and Afra wants Spiky Mike to come and help her control Prometheus because he's gone mad and …'

To her astonishment, Excelsior suddenly crouched down into his take-off position. He sounded serious and grown up. 'Get changed quickly into your flying gear, there's no time to lose. Only another dragon can control a dragon when it's in frenzy. We've got to go and rescue Vincent, and JoJo, we're in a race against time.'

Joanna didn't need telling twice and by the time Spiky Mike arrived at the Brixton Caves, Joanna and Excelsior were already half-way to Brighton.

When Spiky Mike heard what Afra had to say she thought he would explode with anger. 'How can you have been so stupid! I told you this would happen! What do you think I can do against a crazed Jewel Dragon? Or perhaps you want to get rid of me as well!'

Afra shook her head in disbelief, stung by the ferocity of his words. 'No, no! I'd never do anything to hurt you. Can't you see I'm trying to do the right thing?'

Spiky Mike snorted in disgust. 'It's a little late in the day for that! If you really want to do something useful, call Madame Akua and ask for security back up – red alert. No, on the other hand, don't bother. I'll do it – just get out!' He was shouting so loudly that Afra could only stand there stunned. 'I mean it, get out! I can't bear to see you standing there as if none of this were your fault. Well it is!' Afra saw the look of disgust in his eyes. It was too much to bear. She turned and fled. He picked up the phone to call Madame Akua, but the phone was dead. He slammed down the receiver as Agnes came running in to the office. 'Spiky Mike, it's Joanna and Excelsior, they're not in the cave.' Spiky Mike pushed past Agnes, swearing as he went. He knew only too well where they'd gone and he had no choice but to go after them!

Chapter 21

Mortal Combat

Even on a cold grey February afternoon the domed towers of the Brighton Royal Pavilion looked quite magnificent. It seemed exactly the right sort of fairytale setting for a dragon. Excelsior circled round looking for a good place to land. Fortunately the gardens offered plenty of good hiding places.

Joanna slid off Excelsior's back. It was time to put Excelsior's plan into action. They'd talked it through as they'd flown down to Brighton. First Joanna had to find the dragon loading-bay as this would lead directly into the caves. She eventually found the entrance in a side street. It came as a shock to find the doors wide open.

The second part of their plan was for Joanna

to find Prometheus' cave. 'But JoJo be careful! Prometheus mustn't know I'm here so I'll have to make a really strong mind-block, which means you won't be able to contact me either.'

Joanna nodded. 'Look, we've no choice and I promise I'll be as quick as I can.' She slipped inside the loading-bay and made her way into a wide tunnel that spiralled downwards until after about five minutes walking she found herself in a large circular hall. A series of brightly lit passages led off from the hall at regular intervals. It wasn't at all like she'd expected; it reminded her of a laboratory she'd seen on television, all stainless steel, shiny tiles and bright lights. She couldn't imagine dragons liking it at all. She didn't have a clue where to go. The passageways were all colour coded but apart from that they all looked the same. 'Might as well try this one,' she thought, taking the passage immediately in front of her. 'I suppose I'll just have to explore them all until I find the right one.' The passage ended in a doorway, which slid silently open as she approached. It gave her such a shock that she nearly cried out. It turned out to be an empty dragon cave, more like the ones in the Brixton Cave, hewn out of the bare rock. As she stepped back into the passage the door slid shut again. She made her way back to the circular hall and entered the next passage. She had nearly reached the next sliding door when she heard voices on the other side. Should she go back or try and listen? – she might find out where Vincent was being held prisoner. She went as near as she dared. One of the voices was Marius King's! His words made her heart start pounding in her chest. 'If he doesn't do something soon to bring Hannibal round it's going to be too late. I think it's about time we covered our tracks. Have you wiped all relevant data from the Cave computers?'

A man's voice she didn't recognise answered, 'I've wiped the main computer and I've shredded the paperwork from the top-security files, but I can't and won't wipe my most recent research – Marius, you can't make me.'

'Then Frederick, just make sure you've hidden the files where they can't be found,' hissed Marius King. 'Now I think it's time …'

To Joanna's horror the door slid open, and she found herself staring up into the face of Marius King.

'Good afternoon, Ms Morris. How kind of you to drop in here so *un*expectedly.' He stepped back in to the room and to her dismay Joanna saw wall-to-wall screens showing not just security camera images of the corridor where she'd just been standing, but all the caves, entrances and passageways. She frantically scanned the screens and gave a little cry, 'Vincent!' He was slumped against a cave wall. At first she thought he was asleep or worse, then suddenly she realised he was crouched over something very bright, something very white; something she had seen before – the fire! But the flame was so small and it kept flickering and dying out.

Marius saw her quickly scanning the screens. 'Ah, Mr Marlowe is doing a little job for me, and now *you* are here, you can make yourself *useful* too,' Marius King emphasised his words with a cruel sarcastic smile, 'I think one glimpse of you being threatened by Prometheus will be enough to concentrate Mr Marlowe's mind on the task in hand!'

'You wouldn't dare,' shouted Joanna, who was feeling very frightened. This was a man who would dare anything to get his own way.

'Now, you can come quietly, or my friend the doctor here can give you something to make you more amenable,' Marius King's soft voice belied the menace of his words. Joanna shook her head. 'No, I'll come quietly.'

'Oh we are being sensible!' mocked Marius King, adding, 'And don't worry about that silver dragon of yours because after you entered the loading-bay I locked the doors behind you.'

A screen flicked on and Joanna immediately saw Excelsior outside the loading-bay desperately trying to push the doors open. 'Sad really – they open outwards,' laughed Marius King. 'Shall we go?' he added sharply. Joanna had no choice but to do as he said.

Prometheus' cave was at the end of a warren of passages. Joanna knew she would never have found it on her own – not that it made her feel any better. She was desperately trying to think what she'd do when faced with Prometheus.

'Dragon Flyer ...' prompted a small voice in her brain '... Dragon Flyer!'

What did the voice mean? She couldn't fly Prometheus in so small a space ... but she could mind-blend! If she went through the series of mind-blending questions perhaps she would she be able to divert Prometheus' attention away from Vincent? It was all she could think of *to do*. As they approached the door of the cave Marius King grabbed Joanna by the shoulders and pushed her inside.

It was very dark in the cave, except for two pools of light that illuminated Vincent and Prometheus. It reminded Joanna of a Christmas panto; Vincent caught in the tiny spot of silver light from his fire and Prometheus, lying in a pool of deep luminous green that cast strange shadows around the cave. It came as a terrible shock to realise that the dark shadow at the dragon's feet was the crumpled, unconscious body of Hannibal.

'Hey Marlowe – I've brought some inspiration,' shouted Marius King, as he pushed Joanna straight towards Prometheus. The push was all the impetus Joanna needed. She leapt round on to Prometheus' back and before the dragon had time to realise what was happening she had leant forward to begin the mind-blend.

'What are you?'

Taken by surprise, Prometheus answered immediately, 'I am a dragon.'

Instantly she felt Prometheus trying to wriggle out of the mind-blend, but she continued, 'What is your name?' When he wouldn't answer, Joanna reached deeper into his mind with her own. 'What is your name?' she repeated. He was forced to reply, 'Prometheus.'

Automatically she asked the next question, 'What type of dragon are you?'

Out of the corner of her eye she was aware of a bright silver flame. Vincent had already dragged Hannibal clear of the dragon and was now making a flame bright enough to revive him. Prometheus sensed her distraction and tried to take control of the mind-blend. Too late, she found herself staring down into Prometheus' mind. It was vast, a great abyss of fire – flames fanned by his hate, his greed, his power! Did she not know just how much he hated her? Wanted to destroy her? She felt herself slipping down into the consuming flames...

Then suddenly there was an explosion of brilliant silver light and she heard a voice call out, 'I am a Silver Spiked-Back Dragon.'

It took her a moment to realise who it was. 'Excelsior?' He'd done it! He'd got into the caves and had come to rescue her. 'Ask the next question!' came the immediate reply.

'Shall we mind-blend?'

'Yes!'

'Yes!' repeated Joanna automatically. And then like a great silver rope, Excelsior's dragon-thoughts were pulling her back from the brink of chaos until suddenly her mind was free. She found herself falling into a pair of waiting arms that carried her out into the passage. Excelsior had not come alone. 'Joanna, Joanna, can you hear me?' She opened her eyes to see Spiky Mike. She was so astonished that all she could say was, 'How did you get in here?'

'Still had an old security card for the loading-bay. One swipe and we were in. Are you all right?'

She nodded. 'Yes, you can put me down. What about Excelsior?'

She looked past him into the cave. Excelsior was locked in combat with Prometheus; except that the Jewel Dragon was bigger and stronger and was lashing out in all directions with his tail. But what Excelsior lacked in strength he more than made up for in speed and agility – somehow he was always just out of the Jewel Dragon's reach, infuriating Prometheus more than ever.

'Everyone back down the passage, quick as you can!' called Spiky Mike.

Joanna looked around her to see Marius King and Dr Alexander standing at a safe distance from the cave entrance ready to run. Hannibal, although conscious, was still barely able to stand and Vincent was having to half-drag, half-carry him.

'What about Excelsior?' cried Joanna.

Spiky Mike looked straight at Joanna. 'The best way you can help Excelsior is to get out of here as quickly as possible. If I know that dragon he'll only leave when he knows everyone is safely out of harm's way.'

As they hurried into the central hall Joanna

could hear a terrible fury of sound coming from the caves. 'Oh Excelsior PLEASE don't be too brave. We're all...aah...' A pair of strong arms had seized hold of Joanna, pulling her off her feet. Desperately she kicked out with her legs, twisting and turning to try and free herself. 'Let me go! Help! Vincent! Spiky Mike!' she screamed. But it was too late. Marius King slipped a rope around her neck. He pulled it just tight enough for Joanna to feel it bite into her skin. 'Help! Help!' she gasped, as she tried desperately to loosen the rope. But the more she struggled the tighter the rope became. Spiky Mike could only stand there helpless. 'Let her go! Or I'll ...

Marius King's laughter rang round the hall. 'Or you'll what? I wouldn't try anything heroic, not if you want to save this young lady. I only want her for a little while; she's going to be my passport out of here. But if any of you try and follow me I promise you she will die.' He pushed a button in the wall behind him and a lift-door opened. He stepped in, yanking a pale and terrified Joanna in next to him. 'Oh don't worry, I'll send her back down to you. Only by then I will have long gone. Goodbye.' The lift-door slid shut and the lights marking the ascent of the lift flickered on and off in quick succession.

Down the passage the snarl of fighting dragons was coming closer and closer. Vincent, still supporting Hannibal, called over to Spiky Mike, 'Get Hannibal out of here as fast as you can. I'll wait for Joanna. Prometheus is frightened enough of my fire to keep away from me. As soon as the lift comes I'll get in and take Joanna out of the caves that way.'

Spiky Mike nodded. He looked around for Dr Alexander to help him support Hannibal. 'Come on, man – help me. Take some responsibility for your actions!' The doctor was about to run, but turned back and together they shouldered the young flyer out of the hall to safety. Only just in time! Into the circular hall came Excelsior, chased by Prometheus. Behind them the passage collapsed as Prometheus' spiked tail pounded again and again against the walls. The modern part of the caves could not withstand such pressure and was simply buckling and crumbling. But the battling dragons paid scant regard to the great chunks of ceiling and wall that came crashing down around them. They hurled themselves one against the other, coiling themselves around and around each other in a dreadful knot of scales and wing and claw. Vincent could only watch helplessly from the side, praying that the lift would come before the whole hall collapsed around him.

Suddenly the lift-door slid open and there was Joanna, looking pale and shocked. Before she had chance to move Vincent flung himself inside and pushed the button for the upper levels. The lift-doors closed but as the lift slid away Prometheus breathed a great torrent of flame, melting the outer doors. Excelsior went wild. He flew straight at the Jewel Dragon snarling and biting and ripping his wings. Prometheus roared in pain; fire and smoke pouring from his nostrils. He reared up on his hind legs to strike a lethal blow at Excelsior's head. But instead of shielding himself Excelsior hurled his spiked back into Prometheus' soft underbelly. The Jewel Dragon writhed and twisted back and forth as he tried to free himself, but with every twist and turn Excelsior's spikes sank in deeper. Prometheus lashed out desperately with his front claws in a final effort to free himself. But Excelsior was waiting and at the last second he pulled away. Out of the great raw gashes poured blood and gore. Prometheus let out a terrible howl of pain. It was the cry of a defeated dragon. He fell forwards and crashed down on to the floor. The battle was over.

Excelsior turned away. He had no more stomach to stay and watch the death throes of his enemy.

He took to the air and flew out of the hall. Only one question concerned him now. 'Where were Joanna and Vincent?'

Prometheus was dying, but he had one last parting gift to the world. Summoning all his strength he lashed at the walls of the hall with his tail. Hidden behind the tiles were the gas pipes that fed the fires that heated the dragon eggs on the floor above. The tiles smashed on to the floor and he crushed them into powder beneath his feet. Then with a final howl of rage he closed his mighty jaws tightly around the pipes, wrenching them from the walls. All that was needed was a spark …

Chapter 22

To Lay Down One's Life for a Friend

It took all of Vincent's strength to keep Joanna in the lift. In the brief second the lift-doors had opened Joanna had seen Excelsior locked in combat and had wanted to help him. Vincent slammed his hand against the first button he could find. The doors closed and the lift swiftly ascended to the next floor and stopped with a jolt. The doors were stuck and Vincent had to prise them open. They had buckled in the heat and the smell of melted plastic was dreadful. 'It would seem we can't return to the caves below now even if we wanted,' said Vincent, 'and the sooner we get out of this lift the better.' But Joanna didn't move. 'No Vincent, I can't! I've got to help Excelsior.'

'Joanna,' said Vincent quite firmly, 'all we can do is get out of here as quickly as we can. Are you all right? Did Marius King hurt you?' Joanna wouldn't look at Vincent, then mumbled, 'He didn't hit me or anything like that. I'm OK, now please can we go and find Excelsior, I must find out if he's all right.' Vincent took her hand and gave it a gentle squeeze. 'Come on, he'll probably be waiting for us.' He knew Joanna hadn't told him everything, but now was not the time to talk about such things. Together they started to make their way down the passageway. 'We have to try and find an emergency staircase – there must be one,' said Vincent, 'WDRF regulations.' The first door they found unlocked was a laboratory. They were about to leave when Joanna said, 'Look, isn't that a fire-drill notice on the wall?'

'Well done Joanna, glad someone's keeping their head,' said Vincent, pausing to catch his breath. Joanna saw how pale and exhausted he looked. He couldn't have slept for over twenty-four hours. He smiled at her worried face. 'Don't you worry about me – but at my time of life I'm not quite used to so much running about. Now let's have a look at this plan.'

Vincent looked at it very carefully; he wanted to make quite sure he knew exactly where to go. 'Right now we're in Egg Turning Laboratory 3, on the second level down, so the door to the emergency stairs is down the second passage on the ...'

An intense flash of light and a burning heat tore the room in two, ripping through the metal supports that held the ceiling in place. Joanna felt herself thrown across the room – just part of the wreckage of the explosion. Something hard smacked into her and a searing pain seemed to split her back in two. Her legs collapsed under her, and it seemed as though the floor itself was rising up to meet her. She lay there on the floor – at least she thought it must be the floor. She tried to push herself up but found she couldn't move. Vincent – where was Vincent? She tried to call out, but no sound came from her mouth. All she could do was lie still on the floor and try to breathe, but the very air itself was choked with dust; hot dust that burnt and stung her insides. Suddenly there were arms around her, pulling her up, holding her tight and a voice calling, 'Joanna, Joanna! I'm here, hold on to me.' Only there was too much darkness and she couldn't hold on any more.

As soon as he had got out of the loading-bay, Spiky Mike left Hannibal in the care of Dr Alexander and ran round to wait by the lift-doors just inside the main entrance. Surely Vincent and Joanna would be out by now? But he couldn't see them anywhere. Just then the force of the explosion ripping through the caves below threw him off his feet. He heard the crack of bone and his leg gave way beneath him. He had to get up. Joanna and Vincent were still down in the caves! As he tried to stand, a wave of nausea washed over him and he fell to the ground again. Then he was aware of someone standing over him. It was Afra Power. On seeing her, all his anger suddenly surged up inside him and he lashed out at the air with his fist.

'I'm sorry. I'm sorry, please, let me help you.' She bent down, 'Here lean on me.'

'Get away, don't you touch me. Don't you realise Joanna and Vincent are still down in the caves. I've got to help them.' Spiky Mike tried to pull himself up again.

'Down in the caves? But they can't be! I saw Marius just ten minutes ago walking out of this door, he said for now the caves were off limits but that everyone was all right. I've been looking everywhere for you …'

'And you still believe Marius King?' Spiky Mike turned away from her and started to drag himself over to the emergency staircase; his face was contorted with pain and covered in beads of sweat. But Afra went over and stood right in front of him blocking his path

'You can't go! I won't let you! You'll never make it. You'll be killed.'

'Get out of my way,' screamed Spiky Mike.

'You can't go … but *I* can.'

Spiky Mike looked at her in disbelief. Afra held his gaze. 'The worst day of my life was the day you walked out of these caves. I know now that I should have listened to you; perhaps this is my chance to put things right.' And before Spiky Mike could stop her, Afra had opened the door to the emergency stairs and disappeared.

'Afra! Afra!' Spiky Mike called after her. 'Be careful!'

The emergency staircase wasn't part of the modernised caves, and was rarely used. If only it was still clear she had a chance. Afra hurried down the stairwell as fast as she could. The stairs themselves were cut into the rock that had formed the original caves and felt solid and sure under her hurrying feet. She didn't have a clue where Vincent and Joanna would be. She stopped at the first level and ran down the passageway. The emergency lighting was still on, but a section of wall had collapsed, blocking the passageway. Frantically, she called their names again and again. But there was no reply. All right, she'd try the next floor down. She made her way back to the stairs and descended more slowly this time. Cautiously, she opened the door. It was pitch black and she couldn't see a thing. The air was heavy with dust, so she tied her handkerchief over her nose and mouth before making her way along the passage. All around came the loud groans of the slowly twisting metal girders that held together the construction that was the second level of the modern 'caves'. A chunk of ceiling fell down behind her, making her scream. Afra could feel a growing panic inside herself. She was so scared. What if she couldn't find them? If she turned round now and went back no one would blame her. 'But I would blame myself – and how would I ever face Mike again? No. I have to do this … because … I was wrong. And I need to do the right thing because … because I love you Mike and when this is all over' – she had to think *when* not *if* – 'then perhaps I'll have the courage to tell you.'

She continued feeling her way along in the darkness. At last she saw light coming from off the passageway – it must be the opening to one of the laboratories. Suddenly she knew exactly where she was – Egg-Turning Laboratory 3 – the very place where Prometheus had been born! The memory of that afternoon rose up before her. She pushed it away just as she had to push away the broken door and a pile of rubble to get into the room. But then she could only stop and stare. The light she could see came from a small fire; its flames were sharp and silver white, like no fire she had ever seen before. Sitting by the fire was Vincent Marlowe and laying across his lap, still and lifeless, was Joanna.

'I've come to get you out of here,' was all Afra could say, and then looking at Joanna she half-asked, half-sobbed, 'Is she alive?'

Vincent looked up with a gravity that silenced Afra. 'She came to save me, and now I must save her. It's nearly ready.'

Now Afra noticed that Vincent was holding a small beaker over the flames. In it she could see a pale liquid

'What is that … what are you doing?'

'This,' said Vincent, 'is gold dissolved in *aqua regia* – the elixir of life. I can make just enough to save Joanna – but I need silence so that I can concentrate.' Afra squatted down beside him and watched intently as Vincent concentrated all his thoughts on the small glass tube of liquid held in the silver tongue of fire. It reminded her of the concentration needed by a dragon flyer to fly a dragon. Her eyes were drawn to the brightness of the fire and she felt its light pierce her mind. Its brilliant purifying light seemed to scour her very being so that all the hidden thoughts she was trying so desperately to suppress were suddenly laid bare. She turned away unable to withstand such scrutiny. At the same moment Vincent withdrew the small glass tube from the fire and Afra could see that the pale liquid was now golden.

'It's ready; hold Joanna's head so that I can pour it into her mouth.' Afra held back Joanna's head; the girl's body was still and cold. Vincent poured the liquid slowly and carefully into Joanna's mouth drop by drop. Afra willed him to go faster – all around the groans of the twisting iron girders that supported the ceiling were slowly getting louder and louder, but the Alchemist would not be hurried. Finally he looked up. 'The potion will take a little time to work, but there is no time to wait for that. You must take her now.'

Afra picked up Joanna and turned to Vincent. 'I'll go first with Jo …' Then her voice trailed away. He hadn't moved. He couldn't. Joanna's body had hidden the fact that Vincent's legs were pinned to the ground by one of the metal girders. And he was bleeding profusely. He looked at her with a calmness that filled Afra with awe. 'I am not leaving. Unfortunately there was not enough elixir for both of us. As for me, I have lived a good and exciting life; the last few months of which have been the most precious of all. Joanna coming to the caves has been like a breath of fresh air to me; she is perhaps the daughter I never had …'

Afra stared down at him. 'But I can't just leave you. I'm sure I can move this girder.' Afra carefully laid Joanna on the ground then she squatted down and gripping the underneath of the metal girder, she pulled upwards. It barely moved, but immediately the girders overhead groaned and a shower of concrete fell from above, extinguishing the silver fire that had continued to burn, engulfing them in darkness. Afra heard Vincent's insistent voice – 'Stop! You'll bring the whole lot down on top of us. Please you *must* go now, while there is still time.'

Still she could only stand there. 'Mr Marlowe … Vincent … I'm sorry …'

'For what?' he reached up and took her hand. 'You've risked everything today. There is nothing to be sorry for. Now, please go!'

Swiftly she bent over in the darkness and kissed his cheek. '… I wish I could have known you better. I'll do my very best to get her out.'

Afra carefully felt her way in the darkness to where she had laid the still unconscious body of Joanna. Somehow she managed to lift her over her shoulder and with one last glance back at where she knew Vincent lay she stepped out into the passage.

The passage was filling with smoke. She had to get out fast. Joanna was a dead weight but she staggered down the passage barely noticing the ache in her arms. Instinctively she found the handle to the staircase, praying that the air was still clear and fresh. She slammed the door closed behind her and stood gasping for breath before she began the long climb up. Each step became an effort, her legs were shaking with fear and with tiredness but she kept on mechanically lifting one foot after the other until with a final effort – she could hardly believe it – she was at the top. She stood by the top door, steadying herself for a final dash. She could feel her whole body shaking uncontrollably as she pushed open the door and stumbled out into the fresh air, the daylight and life. Behind her there was darkness and smoke and somewhere, trapped underground, the bravest man she had ever known lay dying.

She was aware of the wetness of tears on her face, then of somebody trying to take Joanna from her. At first she refused to let go and clutched the body of the girl closer to her.

'Afra, you need to let go, we need to see if she's all right. You saved her!' Afra was aware that it was Madame Akua speaking to her. Her arms fell limp as the reality of what had just happened dawned on her. 'Madame Akua, Vincent Marlowe ... he's trapped ... I couldn't ... couldn't ... you've got to send someone to help him, quickly before it's too late.' Somebody must have wrapped her in a blanket and given her a sweet hot drink. But she couldn't say who. There were flashing lights and sirens, and people in uniforms moving around, but everything seemed as if it was happening in some other existence.

A team with heavy-duty cutting equipment was dispatched with orders to radio back as soon as they found Vincent. Madame Akua watched them disappear through the doors down into the caves. All she could do now was hope ... and pray. It was a far worse disaster than anything she could ever have imagined. The security back-up team had been impressively fast, but was that now fast enough? Would they find Vincent in time? Each second that passed felt like an hour but then all too soon the rescue team reappeared. It was the worst news possible. All the lower levels were on fire and it was spreading rapidly. They shook their heads. There was nothing they could do.

Madame Akua stood there for a moment as though she was refusing to believe the finality of what they were telling her. How had she been so naïve? Spiky Mike had tried to warn them about Marius King – and they'd all refused to listen. She for one had been well and truly deceived; taken in by his smooth talk and his money. But not any more! She would use every contact, every power available to her to seek him out and bring him to justice. Dr Alexander was already in custody and promising to co-operate fully. Still for now that must wait. Her immediate thoughts must be for the wounded. She pulled herself up tall and walked across to the ambulances where the bruised and dirty group of survivors sat anxiously waiting for news. She could hardly speak the words and turned quickly away to where Joanna was still lying unconscious, oblivious to the tragedy being played out around her. As she watched, Joanna stirred; strange, she looked so peaceful, as though she was just waking up from a good night's sleep.

Joanna opened her eyes. Where was she? How had she got out of the caves? She remembered a flash of heat and the dust as everything came crashing down around her. She vaguely remembered Vincent pulling her towards him. She sat up and looked around. A man in a uniform was asking if anything hurt. 'No, I'm fine,' said Joanna pushing off her blanket as she sat up, 'absolutely fine! See, nothing broken.' She watched in amazement as a stretcher carrying Spiky Mike was lifted into an ambulance. He was soon followed by Hannibal and Afra Power – how had she got there? And where was Vincent? She couldn't see him anywhere. She ran over to the ambulance.

'Spiky Mike, what happened?'

'Joanna, you're all right! Afra saved you …!'

'But what about you?' cried Joanna.

'My leg is broken, but I'm OK.'

'Spiky Mike,' asked Joanna, 'where's Vincent?' Spiky Mike didn't answer her; Joanna could see he had tears in his eyes.

'Where's Vincent?' persisted Joanna. Everyone sat there in silence unable to answer her and suddenly the awful truth began to dawn on Joanna.

'He didn't get out, did he?' said Joanna. Numbness was spreading all though her.

'I'm sorry,' Afra sobbed, 'I tried … he was

trapped. He gave his life to save you, Joanna …
Joanna! Stop! Come back. Someone stop her!'

But Joanna had gone.

Chapter 23

Starlight

Vincent is dead.

I'm not hurt – not even a scratch.

Afra said he gave his life to save me

The thoughts tumbled loosely through her mind. She couldn't think what it all meant – except Vincent was dead!

She ran and ran along the streets of Brighton, not wanting to think or feel until at last she came to the sea. She made her way down on to the stones and walked down to the water's edge. It was just a vast greyness of water; that's what she wanted, just the numbness of grey, instead of this red raw grief that was swallowing up every part of her.

She knew they would be searching for her. The

beach was probably one of the first places they'd look. If only she could get away from them all. Just fly away!

Excelsior!

Where is Excelsior?

He'd risked his life to save them – like Vincent.

Perhaps he is dead too. Killed by that monster.

But Excelsior couldn't be dead; she'd have felt it – wouldn't she? She had to find him. He had to be hiding somewhere.

She tried to think.

The gardens – he would have hidden himself in the Pavilion gardens. She made her way back up to the Pavilion. The cordon set up by the police was still in force, but if she slipped over the wall she could get into the grounds unseen.

She nearly missed him altogether. Quite by chance she tripped over one of his front legs. He had hidden himself in a covering of leaves that had been left to rot.

'Excelsior, it's me, JoJo.'

He didn't answer or move and she sank down next to him knowing his misery was as desperate as his own. They lay side by side as darkness gathered all around them, each lost in their own thoughts until finally Excelsior spoke. 'JoJo, I have done a terrible thing. I have killed one of my own kind. I do not know if I can stand the torment of knowing I have taken the life of another dragon.'

'You killed Prometheus?' asked Joanna – 'Oh, Excelsior you must be proud, not ashamed. Don't you realise that you saved us. If it hadn't been for you we would all be dead.' The word 'dead' seemed to stick in her mouth, forcing her to taste its power. How would Excelsior feel if she told him about Vincent? Would he blame himself for that too?

'No, JoJo, I cannot be proud of what I did. I did what I had to do and now I am changed forever.' Joanna nodded. More than Vincent had died today. Excelsior's innocence, his happy carefree spirit, his fun-loving sweet self, all had been touched by the evil that was Prometheus. 'No,' thought Joanna, 'not just Prometheus, by Marius King!'

'Where is everyone?' asked Excelsior suddenly. 'Are we going home?'

'The others have all gone off to hospital, Spiky Mike broke his leg in the explosion and of course everyone needs checking over to see they're all right.'

'But you didn't go?'

'I ran away!'

'Why?'

Joanna took a deep breath. 'Because ...

Excelsior, Vincent is dead! He gave his life to save mine. I don't know what he did; Afra Power told me. She came and rescued me after the explosion. I ...' She didn't know what else to say.

They dropped into silence. It was dark now. The pale towers of the pavilion had lost their fairytale charm and rose up like great white ghosts come to haunt them. Excelsior was as still as stone; he could have been a statue in the garden, but Joanna could sense a great tension within him. Some inner struggle of which she had no part was taking place within him. Suddenly Excelsior leapt to his feet and spread wide his great silver wings, beating them wildly against the air as though some invisible enemy was attacking him. Joanna leapt away terrified, then it seemed that the moment of crisis had passed for he grew still again. Immediately he turned to Joanna – 'I don't want to stay here anymore. JoJo, let's go home!' – and he began to open his wings in readiness for flight. Terrified he would leave her, Joanna grabbed his neck tightly. 'Don't leave me, XL.'

Somehow she scrambled on to his back and started to mind-blend but her thoughts were as dry and brittle as the dead leaves that lay scattered around them. In contrast Excelsior's response exploded into her mind, nearly overwhelming her. What had happened to him? She felt frail and lifeless beside such power. Almost immediately he lifted his wings and they flew up into the air at great speed. Joanna was so exhausted that it was all she could do to keep the mind-blend.

It was a cold night and despite her flying-suit Joanna was soon freezing cold. But after all that had happened, what did the cold matter? In fact she liked the cold; it was making her sleepy. If she fell asleep perhaps it would all just go away ... She'd just fall asleep for a few seconds ...

But Excelsior was wide-awake. As he felt her hold on the mind-blend slip he reached out with his own mind and held her safe from the pain that threatened to overwhelm her. Slowly, so that she hardly noticed, Excelsior started to fly higher until suddenly they were clear of the clouds.

'Wake up, JoJo!' he called. 'Wake up! I know now that even in the darkest moment there is always hope. I know the worst and I know that it is not the end. Look around you and understand!' Joanna slowly opened her eyes. Above and around in the darkness of the night sky shone thousands of stars, each one a small silver spark of pure radiant light. Strange, she had never noticed before that starlight shone with the same brightness as Vincent's fire. As for Excelsior, he too shone with the same silver brilliance as the stars.

'Did you know, Joanna, that you are made of stardust?' She heard Vincent's voice as clearly as on the afternoon he had told her. It had been their first science lesson. What else had he said? That things were all basically the same. Take away the outer appearance and underneath a dragon wasn't really so different from a human, lead from gold … life from death. 'It is *how* we choose *to live* that makes the difference,' were his words. She had never realised at the time what the reality of those words could mean. Joanna thought of the choices made that day. Spiky Mike, Afra, Excelsior, Vincent: they had all been ready to risk their life to save another.

She gazed at the stars twinkling so brightly. She wondered what it would be like to spend one's whole existence as a burning mass of white light. Did stars ever have to make a choice whether or not to sparkle brightly? Did they ever think or feel?

Suddenly she was aware of Excelsior. Whatever crisis he had battled with down in the Pavilion gardens had passed, but although he was suffering still, something about him had changed; she could feel it in the mind-blend. 'Go deeper,' came a voice that she knew was his but hadn't heard before. Slowly she opened up … not her mind this time, but her heart, and reached out. All around her was the silver light, a light made up of sorrow, pain and … she knew it at once, not happiness but joy. But now it wasn't just inside Excelsior; it was everywhere, surrounding her, holding her, keeping her safe.

'Vincent's fire!' sighed Excelsior.

'Oh,' she gasped, 'it's love, isn't it?'

They flew through the night sky in silence; for neither needed words to express what they felt. And although the pain was still almost too much to bear, their shared awareness of such love both softened and transformed it into a longing for life experienced more fully than it had ever been before.

Finally Excelsior began to descend through the clouds and as he did so the silver light faded leaving Joanna feeling empty and sad but no longer in despair. Down below Joanna could see the steady stream of cars and traffic that filled Brixton High Street whatever the time of day or night and she knew they were nearly home.

'Speaking of love,' piped up the old voice of Excelsior. 'Do you think he's kissed her yet?'

'Whatever are you talking about?' asked Joanna.

'Spiky Mike! Do you think he's kissed Afra yet?'

'Excelsior, how can you ask that now!' cried Joanna

'But it's the *only* good thing to have happened today and Vincent would be pleased,' sighed Excelsior.

*   *   *   *

Of course it was Agnes who was there to welcome them home. She'd sent Joanna's family straight down to Brighton to be with their daughter when she was found and kept a solitary vigil in the caves. Joanna found her sitting in her office. She looked so small and frail just sitting there and suddenly Joanna realised that sorrow had made her old. She pushed open the door and threw her arms around her. 'Agnes!'

'Child, you're safe! Thank God you're safe. We've all been so worried about you. I must phone Madame Akua immediately. Your parents are with her, and they are out of their minds with worry.'

'Agnes, I'm sorry but I couldn't face any of it … Vincent …'

'I know about Vincent,' whispered Agnes. 'Joanna, everyone just wants to know you are safe.'

As she sat there listening to Agnes calmly talking to Madame Akua, Joanna found herself wondering where Marius King was that night and what he was feeling. Regret? Guilt? Or just relief at having saved his own skin! She looked up at the familiar surroundings of Agnes's office. There was her scarf for Excelsior still lying wrapped in its silver paper where she'd left it on the desk. Beside it lay two huge cake boxes tied up with ribbon – Excelsior's birthday cakes. This morning was such a short time ago; could so much have happened so quickly? She wanted things to go back to how they were. She wanted her mum and dad. She wanted …she wanted to go to sleep. All of a sudden she felt so tired. She curled up in Agnes's easy-chair and in less than a moment she was fast asleep.

Agnes put down the phone and seeing Joanna asleep she covered her with a blanket, the same one she had hidden Excelsior in exactly one year ago. The old woman came and sat down beside her, tears now freely flowing down her cheeks. 'Yes, sleep child, for nothing I can do or say will ever bring him back.'

Part 5
AFTERWARDS

Chapter 24

A New Dawn

Madame Akua sat at her desk and sighed deeply. The inquiry was finally over. Dr Alexander had co-operated fully and made all his surviving papers available. The man was obviously a genius, even if he had been misguided. He had always known Prometheus was dangerous but pride in his own abilities had made him believe he had controlled the dragon's mind sufficiently. Pride and of course the promise of further funding to continue his research. And Marius King certainly knew how to persuade. His papers salvaged from the Brighton Caves, revealed forged documents, blackmail threats and bribes. Marius King had hoodwinked them all, herself included. How he must have enjoyed his games of power – must still be enjoying them for it seemed he had disappeared into thin air. Well she'd see him behind bars if it was the last thing she ever did.

She looked through the files. Hannibal had been easy prey for a man like Marius King. Oh, she knew he came across as confident, some said arrogant, but she knew better. An only child, adored by his parents – Hannibal had felt the strain of their ambitions for him. Prometheus was the answer to all his prayers. Guaranteed success. She shuddered; it could have turned out so differently; if it hadn't been for Vincent he would certainly have died.

Poor Afra was still blaming herself for what happened. She didn't see what an extraordinary young woman she was – such bravery; rescuing Joanna like that. At least Afra had more than patched up her differences with Spiky Mike.

She sat for moment thinking about the two caves, Brixton and Brighton – hardly fifty miles apart but they couldn't have been more different. The Brighton Caves were of course closed for the foreseeable future. As for the Brixton Caves; that rather depended on Joanna's parents, for the time being at least.

Madame Akua left the folders on her desk ready

to be filed. She had an appointment to keep; one she was rather looking forward to. She flicked on her intercom – 'Maureen, send in my visitors please, and tell Mrs Metcalfe that I'm ready for her now.'

Mrs Frances Metcalfe was Madame Akua's solicitor. She had been the bearer of surprising news on many occasions, but Joanna and her parents could only listen to her in stunned silence as she read to them from a cream coloured parchment.

This is the last will and testament of Vincent Marlowe, owner of the Brixton Dragon Caves. Being of sound mind and body I, Vincent Marlowe, declare Joanna Morris to be my legal heir. I bequeath to her the Brixton Dragon Caves and all their assets.

If Joanna has not yet reached the age of her majority (18) the caves will be held in trust until that time.

Trustees to be appointed by the WDRF.

Signed *Vincent Marlowe*

'It has been signed, dated and verified by two witnesses. Everything is legal and beyond dispute. All I need to proceed is your consent,' said Mrs

Metcalfe, addressing Joanna's parents. 'There are some additional beneficiaries, Agnes Thomas and Michael Hill in particular, so you have no need to have any concerns for your daughter's colleagues.

Joanna looked from her father to her mother; she was shaking all over.

'Am I to understand that Mr Marlowe has left the caves to Joanna?' stammered Joanna's father, 'I mean, to keep?'

'Yes,' smiled Mrs Metcalfe.

'And the dragon as well?' added her mother.

'Of course,' said the solicitor.

'But we don't know anything about running dragon caves,' exclaimed Anthony Morris. 'Nor are you expected to,' said Madame Akua, 'as the will stipulates, until Joanna is 18 the cave will be run by trustees appointed by the WDRF.'

'And who would these trustees be?' asked Hilary Morris, waving at Joanna to be quiet. 'Joanna, just wait; we have to ask these questions, this is about your future and we have to consider what is best for you.'

Madame Akua smiled. 'I have a here a list of trustees, one of whom as you will see is myself.' She handed the list to Anthony Morris. He looked over it nodding to himself and handed it to his wife saying, 'Looks perfectly satisfactory to me.' Joanna desperately tried to see the list but her mother held it away. 'Joanna, I need to read this carefully.' She looked over the list, and then returned it to Madame Akua with a smile. 'Very good!'

'Don't I get to see, then?' asked Joanna in dismay. 'I can do better than that,' said Madame Akua. 'They're all waiting next door.'

They followed Madame Akua through to a large meeting-room. Sitting around the table were the 'Trustees.'

'I hope you think I have chosen wisely, Joanna?'

Joanna could only nod, she was so happy. Sitting around the table were Agnes, Spiky Mike, Lucia and Giovanni Balivo and (Anthony Morris could not take his eyes off her) Ms Lotty Lupin.

'Spiky Mike and Agnes have also agreed to oversee the general running of the caves, and all major decisions must be approved of by your parents, Joanna. Now I'm sure you want to take this paperwork home to read carefully,' said Madame Akua handing Joanna's parents a large file. 'If you have any concerns, do contact Mrs Metcalfe.'

'Madame Akua,' said Joanna, 'I know I'm still young, but will I have any say in what happens?'

Spiky Mike shook his head as if he'd already given the matter a lot of thought. 'Only if we lay down some clear guidelines. And as I am to remain your trainer for the foreseeable future you must respect that my decision is final when it comes to the discipline of training and other such matters. You see Joanna, I don't know about you,' and suddenly he was grinning at her with the hugest smile, 'I've got my eye not only on Supreme Champion, but on that world speed-record.'

Before the week was over the deeds had been signed and after so much turmoil the normal daily routine finally returned to the caves. And yet nothing was the same. They all keenly felt Vincent's absence, but it was the little things: seeing no light on in his study, the lack of chocolate biscuits in the tin (funny none of them had realised it was Vincent who had bought them) that really made them realise he was gone. But they managed as best they could. Agnes had taken over helping Joanna with her lessons until a more permanent solution could be found and even with his leg in plaster, Spiky Mike had drawn up an extremely detailed training plan to prepare them for the World Championship Speed Trials in San Francisco.

There was one new – and very welcome – addition to the caves. One of the first decisions made by the trustees was the appointment of Afra Power as a second trainer. The new dragon would be born in just over a month's time and Spiky Mike couldn't train Excelsior for the speed trials and oversee the new dragon at the same time. Joanna thought they spent an extraordinarily long time discussing things together in the office they now shared. On Agnes's advice she always knocked very loudly before she disturbed them.

When it came, the Easter race was a real anti-climax, as was the May Day Marathon. Excelsior and Joanna so dominated the races that there was no doubt as to the outcome. Joanna found herself missing the competition Hannibal had given them and realised what a great flyer he had been.

It was the birth of the new dragon that finally helped them all appreciate that life had moved on in the Brixton Caves. Joanna and Excelsior were almost beside themselves with excitement as they watched Agnes take out the egg for its final turning.

'It's going to be a Silver Spiked-Back like you,' whispered Joanna, but Excelsior wasn't listening; instead he was crouching over the egg. Joanna looked again; Excelsior was breathing his own fire over the egg and the flame – could it be possible? – was a silver flame!

'*Spiritus draconis*,' whispered Agnes. 'Of course, dragon's breath! Just as it said in the manuscript. I wonder if Vincent knew …?'

They all stood in silence gazing at the egg bathed in the silver flames, each lost in dreams of their own, until finally small cracks started to appear on the surface of the shell. A few seconds later fragments of shell exploded around them and before them lay the newborn dragon. Excelsior bent over and picking it up in his mouth, he gave it one final blast of flame before he dropped it into the waiting glass tank. It looked like a small miniature version of Excelsior except that its spikes were longer and more delicate. Its body was completely silver whilst the tips of its wings and tail were a shiny black. Suddenly they all sprang into action, talking, laughing and hugging each other.

'It's a girl,' smiled Agnes, 'and look at her weight – 4.2 kg. Vincent would have been extremely pleased.'

'Have you got a name for her yet, Agnes?' asked Spiky Mike.

'As a matter of fact, I have,' replied Agnes. 'There is a saying in the Bible I have thought of often these last weeks: "*Weeping may endure for a night, but joy cometh with the dawn,*" and so the name I have chosen is Aurora.'

'Aurora, the dawn, it's beautiful Agnes,' said Afra.

'A new beginning?' thought Joanna to herself, 'I've just had a really good idea!'

A fortnight later Joanna was sitting at home watching television when the phone rang. 'It's Mouse,' said her Mum. 'At least I think it's her, all I could hear were squeaks.'

'Mouse! Hi ... what ... have I seen *Dragon Fire?* ... it says Hannibal is coming to Brix ... of course I was going to tell you ... no, I don't know how that magazine got hold of it. ... yes, it's fantastic ... of course you can come and visit!'

Chapter 25

JoJo Dragon Flyer

As a way of saying thank you, Marion Claverdale invited Joanna to stay on the Olivers' extensive ranch so that she could make her final preparations for the Independence Day Speed Trials. Both Spiky Mike and Afra would accompany her whilst Agnes would stay in Brixton to look after Aurora; she would be helped by her grandson Isaac. 'I'll be thinking of you though and I'll be watching it all on the television,' she said as she hugged them goodbye.

Nothing was too much trouble for the Olivers and both Hannibal and his mother came to watch the training sessions in case they could offer any advice. The training sessions also gave

Hannibal the chance he wanted to talk to Afra.
'Afra,' said Hannibal quietly, 'I've never said sorry
for ignoring your advice. I won't make the same
mistake twice.'

'We've both had to learn some hard lessons
about ourselves,' replied Afra.

Hannibal nodded. 'I thought I might be jealous,
seeing Jo and XL train for the speed trials, but I'm
not. And if Aurora's anything like Excelsior, I'm
gonna have a great ride.'

'I think she'll be as fast as Excelsior, but much
quieter thank goodness,' smiled Afra.

'Do you know what finally made me decide I
should fly again? It was when Joanna told me that
Excelsior had hatched Aurora's egg in the silver
fire. That fire saved my life ...'

'Vincent's fire,' said Afra, '...that's something
we'll never forget!'

A week before the races were due to start,
Joanna's family arrived. They'd brought with
them two packages. The first was a new jacket
from Ms Lupin. Joanna carefully unwrapped the
jacket from its layers of tissue. On the back of the
jacket under the gold sequins that spelt out her
name was a great flying silver dragon surrounded
by hundreds of rhinestones sewn to look like the
stars of the night sky.

The second was from Madame Akua; only Joanna was not allowed to open it until the morning of the races. She could only wonder what it could be. Her family also had a surprise in store for Joanna. The day before the first race Hannibal drove off with her parents and when they returned they brought with them a visitor.

'Mouse! What a fantastic surprise!' cried Joanna as she watched her friend jump out of the car, with barely a backward glance at the driver!

'It's not everyday that your friend is about to become Supreme Champion!' said Mouse.

'Everybody keeps saying that!' said Joanna. 'But I've seen recordings of Leanne Simpson from the New York Central Station Caves. I think she goes to the gym everyday to work out. She'll be flying an Emerald Snake-Dragon. And then there is a Nigerian flyer, James Nana Owusu-Bonsu. His Golden Spiked-Back Dragon is much bigger and stronger than Excelsior and you should see its wingspan. They're both going to be so difficult to beat.'

'Yes, but you and Excelsior have such a deep mind-blend going that you're in with a real chance.' Joanna nodded; she knew what everybody was saying. What they all expected! It was just since their night flight in the stars mind-blending with

Excelsior had changed so much. *Every* time now she could feel the fire burning within him and it always left her feeling so … ordinary. She hadn't changed, not like he had. And because Excelsior was flying faster and faster, no one had guessed that she was feeling not only left behind but completely useless.

American Independence Day finally arrived and San Francisco awoke to a day of golden sunshine and blue skies; perfect weather for dragon races.

The WDRF Speed Trials always opened with a procession of dragons, flyers and their flags which were then flown in a central arena.

It was only when the Brixton Caves' Flag was raised that Joanna realised what had been in Madame Akua's package. It was a new flag for the Brixton Caves. From the centre of the black and gold flag there now shone a silver star. It was the last flag to be presented and it was left at half-mast whilst everyone stood for a minute's silence as a sign of respect for Vincent Marlowe. Finally the flag was raised to its full height. The competition was about to begin.

It seemed to Joanna that everything went into fast-forward. The races were fast and slick like the dragons around her, but not as fast as Excelsior. He flew. He won. He was like a creature on fire, whilst

Joanna just sat there, letting him do it all until, just as everyone expected, they found themselves in the final facing James Nana Owusu-Bonsu on his Golden Spiked-Back Dragon, Abayomi. The excitement of the spectators was at fever pitch. Who would be Supreme Champion? Television crews and journalists were jostling for photos and interviews from anyone linked with the flyers or their dragons.

Spiky Mike was just finishing one final interview when suddenly the news reporter turned to the camera and said – 'I must interrupt this interview with a news flash.

Marius King has been arrested whilst trying to board a plane in Milan. Our source reports that he is now in the custody of the Italian police. Extradition proceedings are to begin immediately.'

Aware that such news would be spreading like wildfire through the spectators and participants alike, Spiky Mike immediately went to find Joanna. With just a quarter of an hour to go before the final race he presumed she'd be in the pre-race enclosure, but a security guard told him that she had already gone to prepare for the race.

He found her sitting with her back to the dragon. He knew she knew.

'You heard then?'

'Yes.'

'Are you all right?'

'Yes … No.'

'Joanna, what's the matter?'

Joanna nearly didn't say anything, but Spiky Mike just stood there waiting for a reply.

Then, as though a floodgate inside her mind had opened, memories and feelings that she had suppressed came bubbling up to the surface.

'At the inquiry I didn't say everything that happened when Marius King took me hostage in the lift.'

Despite his fears for what she might tell him, Spiky Mike managed to say quite calmly, 'Do you want to tell me Joanna?'

Joanna nodded, and a tear fell down her cheek. Spiky Mike felt a surge of anger against Marius King. Even now his evil seemed to touch and spoil what should be Joanna's moment of glory.

'Marius King told me that I wasn't important, that I'd only done so well because Excelsior was special and that you only tolerated me as a flyer because you knew that in the end it wouldn't make any difference who flew Excelsior. I tried not to believe him, but it's true. You see *so* many people keep on saying it, all the time, look!' She threw down the dragon-racing programme and Spiky

Mike read the article that lay besides Joanna's photograph, '*Plucked from obscurity Joanna was just an ordinary schoolgirl until an extraordinary dragon chose her for his flyer …*'

Joanna snatched back the magazine. 'You see everyone knows it; that all this time it's really been Excelsior doing … everything!'

Spiky Mike took Joanna's hands and pulled her to her feet. As he did, the siren sounded to signal that all trainers should leave so that flyers could prepare for the race. Joanna heard him swear under his breath.

'Look Joanna, I've got to go, if I don't you'll be disqualified. You are no ordinary girl and you are no ordinary flyer.' He stood there for a final moment. 'If you don't believe me, ask your dragon!'

The seconds were ticking by. The siren to start the mind-blend for the speed trial would sound in less than five minutes but she just stood looking at Excelsior, not knowing what to do next.

'Why don't you ask me, JoJo?' said Excelsior.

'I don't know what to ask,' replied Joanna.

'Ask the questions you ask in the mind-blend and I will give you the answers – but for you, not for me.'

'And you'll tell me the truth?' asked Joanna.

'Of course.'

'OK,' sighed Joanna. 'But I'm scared, Excelsior. What if I don't like what you tell me?' She climbed on to Excelsior's back and let her cheek rest against his face.

'All right. What am I?'

'You are a girl,' replied Excelsior.

'What is my name?'

'Your name is Joanna, but my name for you is JoJo.'

Joanna took a deep breath. Here was the question she had been dreading, 'What type of girl am I?'

'You are a dragon flyer.'

'Am I really, XL?'

'Of course you are, don't you remember I told you the first time I ever saw you, when I came down the wall of the town hall?'

'Yes, but why me? How did you know I was a dragon flyer?'

'I heard you calling. And I could tell immediately that you'd be the sort of person I could have fun with, share adventures with. It was obvious you would never try and boss me about to make yourself seem more important. I know *you* think there's nothing special about you, but do you realise NEVER once have you doubted *me*, ever!

You listen, you understand, JoJo, you care. You treat me like a friend! I chose you then and I still choose you now to be my dragon flyer; if it seems ordinary to you it's because it IS what you are! Of course it's up to you. I can't make you believe it; you have to know it for yourself.'

Even if Joanna had been able to put into words what she wanted to say Excelsior didn't give her a chance to reply as he continued, 'Look I *can't* do this without you and as *this is* the moment we've been waiting for it's about time you made up your mind. Only hurry up so that we can mind-blend. I fancy myself as Supreme Champion and I really want a crack at the world speed-record as well. Well, I've got to do something to impress that new dragon, Aurora, or she'll never take me seriously!'

Somewhere close by the siren to start the mind-blend sounded.

Joanna sat there for a moment. It was simple really, like putting the last piece in a puzzle. She just had to be herself – 'JoJo, Dragon Flyer!'

'I'm ready,' she whispered, half to the waiting dragon, half to herself.

She pressed her cheek firmly against Excelsior to begin the mind-blend and realised just how familiar the touch of his scales now felt to her skin. Already Excelsior's thoughts were reaching out to touch hers; she could feel the silver fire burning … only this time she realised it was not only part of Excelsior, it was part of *her*, had always been part of her …

What are you?
I am a dragon?
What is your name?
My name is Excelsior.
What type of dragon are you?
I am a Silver Spiked-Back Dragon
Shall we mind-blend?
Yes.

There it was, the siren announcing the start of the race.

'This is it Vincent, this is for you, for the Brixton Dragon Caves, for Excelsior … and for me!'

FLY!